Crider, Bill, 1941-
Dead on the island.

$18.95

DATE			

© THE BAKER & TAYLOR CO.

Dead on the Island

Dead on the Island

Bill Crider

Walker and Company
New York

First published in the United States of America in 1991
by Walker Publishing Company, Inc.
Published simultaneously in Canada by Thomas Allen & Son
Canada, Limited, Markham, Ontario

Library of Congress Cataloging-in-Publication Data

Crider, Bill, 1941–
Dead on the island / Bill Crider.
p.   cm.
ISBN 0-8027-5787-1
I. Title.
PS3553.R497D38   1991
813'.54—dc20   90-23473
                            CIP

Printed in the United States of America
2 4 6 8 10 9 7 5 3 1

This book is dedicated to the memory of my grand-mother, Antoinette Floyd Brodnax, who loved Galveston as much as anyone I've ever known, and to Bob, Francelle, and Ellen, who will remember all those summer days we spent there a long time ago.

Galveston Island is, for me, as much a state of mind as a geographic location. I therefore apologize to Galvestonians for the liberties I've taken with the island's geography and history in order to make it as much my island as it is theirs.

Dead on the Island

$\triangledown$

1

THERE WAS NO ONE on the seawall except for me and the
rat.

I was there to run; I don't know why the rat was there.
Maybe he just didn't have anywhere else to go. Or maybe he
was looking for a handout. If he was, he'd come to the wrong
place. Even the few forlorn gulls that were floating around
above us knew better.

In the summer it would have been different. The seawall
is crowded then, and it's no good for running, though some
people still try. The tourists are out in force, walking, riding
their rented bikes and pedicycles, dragging their recalcitrant
offspring, cruising along on skateboards, and in general
making the seawall a place to avoid.

Unless you're a seagull, that is. Or a rat.

In the summer, the seawall is rat paradise. The remains
of hot dogs with mustard, corn chips, potato chips, jelly
sandwiches, half-eaten candy bars, parts of pickles, the
leavings of a thousand picnics—it's all there for the taking.

And if you can get your snout into the opening of an
aluminum can, there's the dregs of a beer or a diet Coke to
top off the meal. Then you can slip into a crack in the wall

or into a crevice among the boulders at its base and watch the world go by.

Tanned skin and pasty white; burned and peeling; oiled and leathery—all cinched up in whatever manner of suit might happen to catch your fancy, from a string bikini to a Mack Sennett bathing beauty model from the early days of Hollywood.

But it wasn't summer. It was the last week in February, and a cold norther had managed to push its way down from the panhandle all the way to the coast, dropping the temperature into the lower forties and turning the sky the color of lead. The wind pushed back at the Gulf and moved the heavy clouds along. A frosty mist hung in the air. There were still plenty of beer cans down in among the boulders, but they had long since been emptied of anything a rat might want to drink.

Traffic was sparse on the boulevard, to my left. Today qualified for the depths of winter on the Texas Gulf Coast. It was a day to stay home and read a good book or watch *Jeopardy* on TV.

I wasn't worried about the weather, though. I had on a pair of Nike Air Spans, fleece-lined running shorts, and a black and gray sweatshirt that I'd bought at K Mart. The north wind cut right through the sweatshirt, but I knew I'd get plenty warm once I started the run.

The rat was wearing dark brown fur, a leathery tail, and a quizzical look. I wondered if the wind was bothering him, but before I could ask he disappeared over the side of the seawall. It would be a lot warmer down among the boulders, out of the wind. I hoped maybe he could find an old can of bean dip that might still have a dried brown rim of beans left for him to eat.

I started into the run, going slow at first, not that I ever got up too much speed. I was at the west end of the seawall, running east. I figured to go for a mile or two or three and then turn back, depending on how well my knee held up.

After half a mile I was warming up, and the knee was feeling all right. As long as I held myself to about eight-and-a-half-minute miles it would probably be fine. It was only when I pressed myself that I found myself listing to the right. Even then I could usually keep from falling if I stopped in time, but I told myself there was no need to worry about that. Eight-and-a-half-minute miles were perfectly acceptable.

After about two miles I saw someone coming from the opposite direction. I wasn't surprised, since it was more likely that there would be people in that direction, even in February. It was about time for me to turn around, anyway.

I was about to make my turn when I recognized the other runner, even though he was a good way off. You can do that, recognize runners from their gait. Me, for instance. I have a sort of modified version of the Ali Shuffle, except that it's all forward motion. My feet don't ever get too far from the ground. Can't afford to jar the knee.

The runner up ahead wasn't like me in the least. He was getting his knees up and moving right along, smooth and steady. Probably hitting the miles in seven minutes or a little less. I'd've bet a dollar it was Raymond Jackson.

So I didn't turn around, after all. Later, I wished that I had, but he would just have caught up with me. There was a time when . . . but that was quite a while ago.

When we met, Raymond turned and slowed to my pace. "What's happenin', Tru?" he said

"Nothing much, Ray," I said. Ray's a black man, late thirties or thereabout. My age. He's about the size of a good NFL defensive back, but he looks to be in better shape than most of them. "How's it with you?"

"Not bad," he said.

We ran along together for a few minutes. I was breathing a little harder than he was.

When we got to the three-mile mark, I said, "I'm turning

it around, Ray. Good to see you." I sprinted out ahead and
made an easy, wide turn.

Ray turned, too. "I'll go along with you for a ways," he
said.

Neither one of us was inclined to talk much, so we ran in
silence for a while. The scudding gray clouds, the mist, the
gray-green water of the Gulf—all of them together didn't
seem to make it much of a day for talking.

Finally Ray spoke up. "Dino wants to see you."

I'd been afraid all along that running into Ray hadn't been
a coincidence, though I'd hoped it was.

"What for?" I said.

"He's lost somethin'. He wants you to find it," Ray said.

"I can't do that anymore," I said.

"Hey, I know that," Ray said. He wasn't having any
trouble talking at all. I was having to pause a little between
every second word. "I told Dino that. I said, 'Man, he don't
do that kind of job anymore.' Dino just looked at me. You
know how he does. 'He'll do this one,' he said. 'Find him.'
So I found you. I hope you not gonna make me look bad and
not talk to him."

We ran on for a minute or two. "I'll talk to him," I said.
"Thanks for making it look like I had a choice."

Ray laughed, but he didn't say anything. We ran along
until we got nearly to the end of the seawall, where my car
was parked.

"You don't put up much of a front, man," Ray said. He
was probably talking about my car, a '79 Subaru GL with
two doors and fading gray paint that just about matched the
color of the day.

"It gets me where I'm going." I opened the door and
reached into the backseat, where I usually have a couple of
towels. I threw Ray a green one and kept the yellow one for
myself. It's softer.

I stripped off the sweatshirt and dried off as best I could

in the cold mist. I put on another sweatshirt from the backseat.

"Sorry I don't have another one," I told Ray.

"That's all right," he said. "Just give me a ride up to my car."

We scrunched ourselves into the Subaru and started up Seawall Boulevard toward the east end of the Island. "About Dino," I said, shifting through the gears. "When?"

"Today's fine," Ray said. He had my green towel draped around his neck. "You wanna come by after lunch?"

"Two o'clock?"

"Two o'clock it is. I'll tell him. There's my ride."

We were almost to the Moody Center, which had been the Buccaneer Hotel when Ray and Dino and I were young. From buccaneer to retirement home. There was probably a message somewhere in that for me if I let myself think about it. I didn't let myself.

Ray's car, a maroon BMW, was parked across the street from the Moody Center. I stopped by it.

"I didn't know you'd become a yuppie, Ray," I said.

He got out of my car and leaned in to toss the green towel into the backseat. He grinned. "Yep, well, it just goes to show you never can tell."

I laughed.

"Two o'clock," he said. "Don't you forget, now." He shut the door and the window rattled a little bit.

"Yeah," I said to myself, driving to the corner and turning left. "Two o'clock."

I was living that year in a two-story unrestored Victorian house not far from St. Mary's Hospital on Avenue I. Or on Sealy Street. Call it either one; that's what the locals do. I get mail just the same, though it's mostly addressed to "Occupant."

For a long time, Galveston seemed determined to destroy

all the relics of its historic past and was doing a damned good job for the most part. Now the buildings on The Strand, some of them anyway, have been restored to their former glory, and a lot of the Victorian houses in the historical district are looking better than they have for over a hundred years. The trim sparkles, and the pastel paint jobs, inspired by *Miami Vice* most likely, would turn Sonny Crockett puce with envy.

The place where I lived didn't look that good.

I wasn't exactly in the historic district anyhow, and the guy who owned the house was just holding on to it as an investment. Which meant that he was paying the taxes and hoping that someone would come along and offer him a whopping profit for it. In the meantime I was serving as a sort of glorified house sitter, supposedly making sure that thieves didn't break in to steal and vandals didn't corrupt the investment.

I drove into the alley behind the house and parked in the backyard. There was no carport, but I had a cloth cover I could toss over the Subaru in case of storms. I climbed the outside stairs of the house to the second floor. The first floor was used mostly for storage, and it would take a lot of work to get it back as it had looked in the previous century. The original hardwood flooring was still there, but not much else.

Upstairs wasn't that much better. I'm not known for my neat housekeeping, and the furniture hadn't been approved by anyone's decorator. In fact, most of it was cast-off items that I'd picked up from friends or found lying in the streets. The sofa was missing a cushion, the recliner wouldn't recline, and the old RCA color set insisted that most of the people on TV these days had a vaguely green cast to their skin. It also had a nearly round picture tube. I didn't particularly care. I also had an old Voice of Music portable hi-fi record player that I could play my 45s on. It sat on the floor by the sofa.

There was a real brass bed in the bedroom, but the mattress sank in toward the middle and was probably as old as the bedframe, not that I minded.

Most of the rest of the furnishings were books, paperbacks mostly, stacked haphazardly by the couch and the chair and the bed. I was reading Faulkner then, straight through, starting with *Soldiers' Pay* and working my way up to *The Reivers*. It passed the time.

There was an old chiffonier by the bed, and there was a picture of my sister, Jan, on it. I kept it there just to remind me.

Nameless was lying in the middle of the bed. He's an old orange tomcat who is totally unrefined and doesn't really care where he lies down. The couch, the bed, and the recliner are all the same to him. He comes in most every day, and since he can't read, or so he pretends, he passes the time sleeping. He lets me feed him if I behave myself.

I hadn't intended for him to be nameless. When he first came in I tried various names on him—Sam, Leroy, Elvis—but nothing seemed to fit. Besides, I didn't really expect him to take up permanent residence. By the time he did, I'd run out of names. So now he was just Nameless.

Nameless looked at me through slitted eyes as I came in, then ducked his head around and tried to shape himself into a ball.

"Don't worry," I told him. "I'm not going to roust you." I threw the towels and sweatshirt I was carrying into the corner by the chiffonier and then stripped off what I was wearing and added it to the pile. There was an old Maytag washer on the first floor that still worked pretty well. I'd take a load down later.

I went into the bathroom and took a shower, first hot, then cold. The bathroom had been modernized about twenty years before, and the plumbing still worked just fine. I toweled off, dressed in jeans and yet another sweatshirt, this one with a red Arkansas razorback on it, and looked for something to eat.

There was a kitchen where another bedroom had once been. The kitchen had been installed at about the same time as the bathroom, but the appliances had not been new even then. The freezer compartment in the refrigerator was about the size of a cigar box. I found some bread that wasn't moldy and made a peanut butter sandwich.

I sat in the recliner and tried to read *Absalom, Absalom* while I ate. Every now and then the knee would twinge, just to remind me that I'd been running. My mind kept drifting off the book and I had to drag it back forcibly. After a while, I went to sleep.

▽

2

SOMETIMES I HAVE TROUBLE sleeping at night, and it catches up with me. I woke feeling a little stiff from having dozed off in the chair, and I was sorry I hadn't rousted Nameless from the bed earlier.

I checked my black plastic Timex. It was one-thirty, leaving me plenty of time to get to Dino's. I wondered what it was he wanted me to look for. Or who. I wasn't sure I could be persuaded to do it, even by Dino.

I put a couple of 45s on the Voice of Music's thick changing spindle, "Ruby Baby" by the Drifters and something by Ricky Nelson, and tried to read a little more of the Faulkner book. I got through a page or two before it was time to leave.

I went into the bedroom and gathered up Nameless, no small job considering that he must've weighed eighteen pounds or so. I carried him down the stairs and set him in the yard. He didn't object, but he didn't look too pleased with me, either. He watched sullenly as I got into the Subaru.

Dino didn't live far, but then nothing is far from anything else on the Island. His neighborhood was a long way removed in time from mine, though. A hundred years ago, people built their houses high to get the afternoon breeze off the Gulf and maybe even to take a look out at the surf every now and again. Then, thirty or forty years ago, the natives, the ones who called themselves BOI for Born on the Island, went the other way and built houses that looked like houses anywhere and tried to deny that the water was even out there.

Dino lived in a big Georgian-style house that would have looked right at home in one of the older neighborhoods in West Texas, Abilene or San Angelo, and up and down the street there were similar stodgy brick houses pretending that they were built on solid rock instead of shifting sand.

There were people on that street who never wet a toe in the Gulf. Some of them probably hadn't even *seen* the water in years.

I parked on the street and went to the door. Ray opened it before I could ring the bell.

"Come on in," he said. "Dino's in the living room."

Dino's living room was nicer than mine, but the furniture hadn't changed since the 1950s, except for the entertainment center, which must have held every electronic device known to the video trade. There were a huge, flat-screened TV, a VCR, a videodisc player, stereo speakers, and a couple of items I couldn't identify.

Dino was sitting on a floral-covered sofa watching *General Hospital*. "This shit hasn't been the same since Luke and Laura split," he said. He turned off the set with a complicated device that was about the size of a paperback book and had more buttons on it than a doorman's coat. "How's it hanging, Tru?" He got up and offered me his hand.

"It's fine, Dino," I said. "You're looking good." It was true. He was still solid and hard, like the linebacker he had once been.

"I still work out," he said. "I hear you do, too. I could never do that running stuff, though. I pump a little iron. How's the knee?"

I looked over at Ray, who smiled. "It's OK," I said. "I get around all right. Ask Ray."

"That's right, Dino," Ray said. "The guy nearly ran me into the seawall today."

"I bet," Dino said. "Well, let's sit down. Get us some drinks, Ray. What'll you have, Tru?"

"You got a Big Red?"

Dino made a gagging sound. "I got it. I knew you were coming over. Bourbon and Seven for me, Ray. Big Red. Jesus." He sat on the sofa.

I went to an overstuffed straight chair nearby. "What's the deal?" I said.

"Let's wait for Ray," he said. So we waited.

Dino and Ray and I went back a long way. We grew up together on the Island, though in different parts of the town. When the Island had been wide open, which it had been until the mid-1950s, a couple of Dino's uncles had controlled all the gambling and most of the prostitution. I didn't remember anything about that time, having come along at the tail end of it, but I'd heard plenty. You couldn't grow up on the Island and not hear. Ray had been born in one of the black whorehouses, and somehow one of the uncles had gotten to know him (or maybe it was Ray's mother whom he got to know). Ray had been brought up practically like a member of the family. Me, I was just another guy, until high school, when I have to admit in all modesty that I became the best damned running back that Ball High had ever known. My ability on the field got me inside a lot of doors that would have otherwise been slammed in my face, and Dino had been on the team.

Ray came in with the drinks. "I forgot you liked yours out of the bottle," he said, handing me a glass of Big Red and a napkin.

"I'll manage," I said, taking the glass and wrapping the napkin around it.

"So, Tru, how long you been back on the Island," Dino said, sipping at his drink. "A year now? Little more?"

"About that," I said.

Ray had left the room again. He hadn't had a drink for himself. I took a swallow of the Big Red. Some people say it's like drinking bubble gum, but I like it. I figured Dino would get to the point eventually.

"You think you'll be staying?"

"It's a thought," I said.

"You got any money?"

"A little. I've been painting a few houses. Not too many lately, though. But business will pick up in the spring."

"I got a little job you could do," Dino said, twirling his glass between his palms as he leaned forward on the sofa. "You could make a little money before spring."

I took another swallow of Big Red. "What's the job?"

"I want you to find somebody," he said.

"I don't do that anymore."

Just about then Ray walked back into the room. "That's what I told him," he said.

"Yeah, but I figured that was just bullshit," Dino said. "You aren't the kinda guy who'd just quit like that. Not you."

"Sure I am."

I set my glass down on the floor. There was a coffee table that had legs that started somewhere in the middle and curved out to the edges and were tipped with something that looked like copper claws, but it was too far away to reach.

"Look," Dino said. "I knew Jan, too. I liked her. Ray knew her. He liked her. Everybody liked her. Nobody blames you. You got to get over that."

"Why?" I said.

Dino put his glass on the coffee table, got up, and started pacing around. "It's not your fault she disappeared," he said. "It's not your fault you couldn't find her."

"He's right," Ray said. "Maybe she just wanted to disappear. She may turn up any day now with a story about spending a year in Vegas."

"No," I said.

"OK, probably not," Dino said. "I got plenty of contacts in Vegas. I checked that one out."

"That was just sort of an example," Ray said. "She could be anywhere."

"She's dead," I said. "We all know that. We just don't know who did it, or why, or what he did with her."

Dino sat back down on the couch. "OK. OK. Maybe so. But that's no reason for you to fold it up. You can't just lie around and paint houses when you get the chance. I checked you out, too. You had a good thing going when you were a P.I. You could find anybody."

"I couldn't find my sister," I reminded him.

"Let me put it this way, then," Dino said. "You owe me one. I called in a lot of markers to help you look for Jan."

"Yeah," I said. "I know. I owe you one."

"Besides that, I . . . what'd you say?"

"I said, 'I know. I owe you one.'"

"That's what I thought you said. You mean it?"

"I mean it," I said. "You helped me out, and you didn't have to, not even for old times' sake."

Dino laughed. "That knee still bothers you, huh? Well, I didn't help on account of that. You were a buddy, and you needed help. So I helped. It didn't work out, but I tried." He picked up his glass and tried to take a bite off one of the ice cubes that was left. "So, you gonna help me with this one?"

"Maybe. Tell me what it is, first."

"I don't think he trusts you, Dino," Ray said. He was standing somewhere behind me.

"It's not that," I said. "It's just that you might be asking something that I really can't do. Or won't do. So tell me who you want me to find."

"Get the picture for him, Ray," Dino said.

I didn't hear Ray leave the room, but he must have. In a minute he was back, holding a cardboard folder. The outside of the folder had a sort of wood-grain look, just like the folders we'd gotten our own high school pictures in twenty years before. Ray handed me the folder.

"Take a look," Dino said. I opened the folder. Inside was a five-by-seven color glossy of a girl about sixteen or seventeen. Straight hair, the color we used to call mousy blond. Blue eyes, a strong nose, a firm mouth. She had a prettiness about her, but there was nothing fragile in it.

"So," I said. "A nice-looking kid. She the one that's missing?"

"That's right," Dino said. "Two days now."

"And you want me to find her."

"Right again. No wonder you were such a hotshot investigator."

"No need to be touchy," I said. "Whose daughter is she?"

"A friend's," Dino said, looking at his empty glass.

"That won't get it," I said. "If I do this little job for you, and I'm not saying I will, I'll have to talk to her parents. Kids disappear for a lot of reasons. Some of them are right at home."

"Not this kid," Dino said. "Take my word for it."

I handed the folder back to Ray. "This isn't going to work," I said.

"Goddammit, Tru!" Dino jumped to his feet.

I stayed in my chair. "Look, Dino, I work the way I work. In a case like this, I always talk to the parents. Besides, it's bound to be complicated. I'm sure you've already tried a few things yourself, like you did for me."

"Tell him, Ray."

"We've checked with the cops," Ray said. "We've put out feelers in other cities where we still have contacts. I've been to the bus station here and in Houston. And in a few towns in between."

"What'd you find out?" I said, but I figured I knew.

"Not a goddamn thing," Dino said. "Not one solitary goddamn thing. The cops don't know from nothing. Nobody's seen her. She's just gone. Just like—"

"Like Jan," I finished for him. "You can say it. I won't mind."

"She's younger than Jan," Ray said. "It's not the same thing."

I could have told him that he was making a mistake right there. You never assume anything. If you do, you mislead yourself. But I didn't tell him. Instead, I said, "What about her friends? Teachers? Does she work? When was she last seen? I've got to talk to her parents and find out things like that."

"*I* can tell you," Dino said.

"This is beginning to smell," I said. "I don't think I want to be involved in it, even if I owe you." I stood up.

"You're gonna have to tell him, Dino," Ray said.

"Shit," Dino said. He looked at me hard and then said, "All right, goddammit. Sit down. I'll tell you."

I didn't move.

"Please," Dino said. "Please sit down. Is that polite enough for you? You want pretty please with sugar on it?"

I sat down. Ray handed me the folder again.

"There's not any parents," Dino said. "I mean, there's not any father. The mother is one of my uncles' girls."

I looked at Ray.

"He's telling it, not me," Ray said.

"She stayed in town after the houses closed down," Dino said. "Nobody knew where she'd worked before, and she's a respected woman now. She had the kid a few years after leaving the houses but before she'd really established herself. She was naturally a little upset at the idea that part of her past might come out in an investigation, and she asked me to see what I could do."

"Another favor from big-hearted Dino," I said.

"Yeah, another favor. Nothing wrong with that. We take care of our own, you know?"

"I know."

"I know a few people on the cops," Dino said. "They didn't ask to see the parents." He gave me a hurt look.

"They don't work like I do. They've got computers and terminals everywhere, which is good in a way, but it keeps them from doing some of the legwork they used to do."

"Well, Evelyn—the mother—didn't want to talk to them, and she didn't have to. I guess she'll talk to you, but you gotta promise that you won't talk to anyone about her past, uh, occupation.

"No promises," I said. "I don't really want to do this."

Dino looked at me for a second or two. "Go call Evelyn, Ray. Tell her the deal. See what she has to say."

Ray faded out of the room again.

"This Evelyn have a last name?" I said. "A job?" I opened the folder and looked at the picture again. "I'm just curious, but I'm going to have to know sooner or later. Why not now?"

Dino walked back over to the sofa and sat down. He picked up the button-covered TV control and turned it over and over in his hands. "Her name's Matthews," he said finally. "Evelyn Matthews. And, yeah, she's got a job. She works at the medical center as a receptionist. I don't think she's going to want to talk to you there, though."

Ray came back into the room. I didn't hear him coming, but there he was. "She'll talk to him," he said. "But she's not too thrilled about it."

"That's just because she hasn't seen me yet," I said.

Dino smiled faintly. "I forgot what a high opinion you had of your looks. But somehow I don't think you'll impress this one."

"We'll see. When and where?"

"Her house," Ray said. "After she gets off work. I'll write down the address."

This time he was back quickly. He handed me a piece of white paper with the address written in black ballpoint. It was just off Ferry Road.

"Easy enough to find," I said. "All the streets over there are named after fish, though." I looked at Ray and then at Dino. "There're probably a few more things you guys want to tell me now."

"Huh?" Dino didn't get it.

"I mean, you must've found out something about the girl, maybe something I should know. You must've done a little nosing around here in town."

"Oh," Dino said. "Yeah. We did that. A little. But it's your turn now. Maybe we did it wrong, and anyhow, everything we know, we got from Evelyn. If you're gonna talk to her, you can get everything we got. After that, it's up to you. You're the ace private eye."

"Your faith in me warms my heart," I said. "Especially considering my track record around here."

"Look, Tru," Dino said. "You gotta quit blaming yourself. We told you it wasn't your fault."

"I know. I just can't convince myself."

"Well, this may help you get it off your mind. Working for somebody else, I mean."

"Maybe." I didn't believe it any more than he did.

"Sure it will. Now, what's the freight?"

"It's a favor," I said. "Like you did for me."

Ray laughed somewhere behind me. "How much money you got in the bank, Tru?"

I turned my head so I could see him. "A little."

"I bet 'little' is just the right word," he said.

"I never thought house painting was going to make me rich."

Dino stepped over to my chair. "I want this official, and

I want your best shot. What do you usually charge? Two hundred a day and expenses? Tell me if that's not enough."

"Well," I said, "it beats painting houses."

He reached into the pocket of his wool-blend slacks and pulled out a sheaf of bills folded in half. He counted out ten of them. "Here's for five days, not counting the expenses. You can keep a record or not. I'll trust you on them."

I took the money. It had been a long time since I'd held that much. "What if I don't find her? I looked for Jan hard for six months, a lot of the time for three more, and off and on for the last three. I still haven't found a trace."

"You get paid for doing the work, not for the results," Dino said. "Besides, this is just a kid. This is different."

"Sure it is," I said. I stood up. "I'll be in touch."

$\triangledown$

3

From dino's house i cut back to Broadway and drove toward the beach. There's a lot of Galveston's history along Broadway. The wide esplanade is covered with oleander bushes and tall palm trees and often looks quite pretty, but on either side of it are the signs of what's become of a once-beautiful city.

The long cotton warehouses of the old compresses, once jammed with bale after bale of cotton, stand deserted and empty. It's a polyester world, but the cotton shipping had long departed Galveston before people started dressing in miracle fibers. Signs of decay are all around. A huge hardware store, empty, its windows boarded up, its parking lot cracking and weeds growing through the cracks. An old movie house that's gone through every phase there is. Not so long before it had been showing *Debbie Does Dishes*, and now it was trying to make a go by showing G-rated family films. Muffler shops. Pawn shops.

But on down the street are Ashton Villa and the Bishop's Palace, once a private home that would knock your eyes out if you could see it in the middle of a lavish country estate instead of cramped up between other houses of a less noble appearance. Galveston had once been the most powerful and richest city in Texas; now it was a vestige.

I turned over to The Strand, named for the famous London street. This was where the town was really making its comeback, restoring the old buildings and regaining some of the grandeur of the past with the Tremont House and the 1894 Grand Opera House.

I drove on down to the medical center, one of the few things in Galveston that Houston hadn't managed to steal. The wonderful old main building, Old Red, was still there, but it was hardly visible from the street, thanks to all the new buildings that surrounded it and almost hid it from view. Evelyn Matthews worked somewhere inside the complex, but she had said that she wanted to see me later, at her home, so I wouldn't bother to stop.

I had a thousand dollars in my billfold and what appeared to be an unlimited expense account. Whatever she wanted was fine by me.

I drove on up Seawall Boulevard and down to the South Jetty. The area was deserted, thanks to the weather, which had not improved a hell of a lot since my run that morning. I didn't mind. I liked having the jetty to myself, and I didn't feel too cold in the sweatshirt. The wind had died down somewhat, but the sky was still gray and low, the temperature still hovering in the forties.

I parked the car and walked out on the jetty, which was basically just a pile of granite boulders with the Gulf water sloshing around them. It was fairly smooth walking if you kept to the middle, but the edges were just a jumble. The granite had been hauled in on railroad flatcars, and the railroad had been built right on top of the jetty while the jetty got longer and longer. The engines had backed the flatcars right into the Gulf, so to speak.

About halfway out I sat down and thought about Jan. Black hair, brown eyes that laughed all the time. White teeth, just the least bit crooked. The kind of kid sister that could keep up with her older brother when he climbed a tree or rode his bike.

She'd disappeared at just about this time of year, or a little earlier. I'd missed her letters for a couple of weeks, and it was unusual for her not to write. So I called. No answer. I'd called back every few hours for two days; then I'd gotten into the Subaru and driven to Galveston. Her apartment had been neat but empty. There was dust on the tables and knickknacks. There hadn't been anyone there for a while. There was no note, no message, nothing. She was just gone.

I'd gotten in touch with some old friends, including Dino. I'd talked to her co-workers, her friends, anyone who might have known her. They were no help. Neither were the cops.

I waited. No credit card bills came in. There were phone calls, but just from people wanting to know where the hell Jan was. I couldn't find her car. The cops couldn't find any trace of it in their computer records of arrests or accidents.

It was as if she'd just vanished into the Gulf breeze.

There was nothing unusual about a woman vanishing, God knows. It happens every day, and probably several times a day, in and around a city like Houston, and Galveston is certainly a part of the greater Houston area, no matter how much it galls the BOIs to admit it. Sometimes bodies and bones are found months or years later by some kid playing in a field or taking a shortcut home from school. It makes the news for a day or two. Then everyone forgets.

I showed her picture everywhere. In the places I knew she went, in the clubs and dives, in the shops and the corner groceries. Nothing. No one knew a thing, no one had seen her. For six months of hard looking, nothing. And all the time after that. Nothing.

Dino was right. I'd quit the business for a year, obsessed with my own search, and I'd found nothing. It was time for me to get back to trying to find something for someone else. Just to see if I still could.

But I knew I was never really going to stop looking for Jan.

A woman and a small boy came out on the jetty. She was holding his hand. A gull flew down by them hopefully. The woman had on a long cloth coat, and the boy had on one of those iridescent jackets that looks sort of like a life jacket with sleeves. They were carrying a sack of popcorn, and the boy started tossing it into the air a piece at a time. He couldn't get it high enough to interest the gull, but his mother took over, and pretty soon there was a wheeling and screeching flock all around them. The boy was laughing and the gulls were swooping close enough to snatch even his clumsy tosses out of the air.

I thought about the rat. Too bad he was at the other end of the seawall. He would have enjoyed the popcorn.

After a while the woman and the boy left. The gulls hung around and picked up a few of the puffy bits lying on the jetty. Then some of them flew over to where I was sitting in hopes of picking up something else.

"Forget it, gulls," I said.

They weren't bothered in the least by my voice, and they screeched and swooped for a few more minutes before they gave up and went back to whatever it is they do when they aren't begging: sitting on posts, floating on the swells, scouting out new territory. Eventually I got up and went away myself.

I killed a little more time walking around on the beach, looking for shells. Sometimes in the winter you can still find them, but not very often. Certainly not like when I was a kid and it seemed as if they were lying everywhere.

When I figured that Evelyn Matthews had had plenty of time to get home from work, I got in the car and drove over to her house.

It was easy enough to find, once I located the street among

the Tunas and Mackerels and Dolphins. The house was just like all the other houses in that area; they looked as much alike as if they'd been stamped out with the same die. Frame structures with one-car garages, all part of a cheap and quick development a long time ago, but all well kept up and nicely painted now.

I parked the car, went up the walk, and knocked on the door. I didn't see a doorbell button.

I didn't know what I was expecting to see, but the woman who answered the door wasn't it. I suppose that I'd associated her working for Dino's uncles with the time of their heyday, which began in the 1920s and extended into the 1950s. Let's face it. I was expecting some kind of little old lady, but the woman who answered the door looked no older than I did.

She was short, with dark hair and eyes, and her figure was what might best be described as voluptuous. She'd probably really been something thirty years ago.

"You must be Truman Smith," she said. Her voice was dark, like her hair.

"That's right," I said. Before she could ask, I took out my billfold and handed her my ID. She looked it over and handed it back. Only then did she ask me inside.

We walked into a small living room furnished with a love seat instead of a sofa, a couple of platform rockers, and a twelve-inch TV on a stand. There was also a small bookshelf against one wall, and I drifted over to it. I'm incorrigibly curious about what people read. There was no Faulkner, so there was no danger we'd be involved in a literary discussion. Her taste ran more to Bobby Ann Mason and Margaret Atwood.

"Have a seat," she said, and I sat in one of the rockers, which was covered with some sort of Early American pattern: lanterns, plows, harnesses.

"Truman," she said. "That's a funny sort of name. Is it a family name?"

"No," I said. "It's a political name. My father always liked that picture of Harry Truman holding up the newspaper headline declaring Dewey the winner of the 1948 election. He liked to see the underdog win."

"Oh," she said.

"Most people just call me Tru," I said.

"All right, Tru." She looked at me with her dark eyes for a minute as if making up her mind about something. "Dino says I can tell you everything. He says you won't involve me in any way that might . . . might . . ."

"I won't compromise your position in town, not if I can help it," I said.

"That's what I mean, I guess."

"Then don't worry. Dino and I grew up together, played a little football together. He was a couple of years ahead of me in school, but we know each other pretty well. If you trust him, you can probably trust me."

"I'll try," she said. "Do you mind if I smoke?"

It was her house. I was so surprised that she'd asked, I said "no" before I thought about it. She got up and went out of the room, then came back carrying a table that looked a little like a TV tray. She set it down by her chair, and I could see a package of Marlboro Lights on it, along with a Bic disposable lighter and a pink ceramic ashtray shaped like a scallop shell.

She tapped a cigarette out of the pack and lit it with the Bic. She inhaled deeply and blew the smoke out in a long, straight jet. I don't really mind smokers, and in fact she made smoking look so good that I was tempted to take it up myself.

"What do you need to know?" she asked.

"Let's start with you," I said.

"Me? But I thought—"

"You thought this was about your daughter, and it is, but Dino didn't tell me much, and I want to get a feel for things. So we'll start with you. For one thing, you're a lot younger than I expected. That is, if you worked where Dino said you did."

She smiled behind a cloud of smoke. "I'm forty-six."

She looked a lot younger than that. "Still, I would've expected someone around fifty. Maybe older."

She tapped her cigarette on the edge of the ashtray. "You're sure you want to hear this?"

"I'm sure."

"All right. I came down here when I was fourteen years old. I wanted to be a whore." She looked at me to see if I was shocked. I wasn't, so she went on. "I was from Houston, and I'd heard about the houses here. Where I lived, you heard about places like that."

"You hear about places like that everywhere," I said.

She tapped the cigarette again. "I guess that's true. What I mean is that where I lived, places like that seemed like an attractive alternative. Anyway, I hitched a ride to Galveston and showed up at one of the houses on Postoffice Street. There's always a market for girls of fourteen."

I did some quick arithmetic. "You couldn't've worked for very long. The last of those places closed in 1957."

"Technically, you're right. But for a young, attractive girl there was still an opportunity for some free-lance work at certain hotels. I didn't have anywhere else to go, and I needed the money, so I was able to keep working for a while."

I'd brought the folder Ray had given me, and I handed it to her. "Where does your daughter come into this?"

She opened the folder. "Her name is Sharon. Didn't Dino tell you?"

I shook my head. "Dino didn't tell me anything. I wanted to hear it from you."

She held the folder in her left hand, looking at the picture. In her right was the stub of the cigarette, which she ground out in the ashtray. "This picture was taken a few years ago, her senior year in high school. She's nearly twenty now."

I did some more figuring. Sharon had been born when her mother was twenty-six, twelve years after she'd come to the Island. "Were you still, ah . . . ?"

"Whoring? The word doesn't bother me. I just don't want people to know for Sharon's sake. Yes, I was. I'd been on the southwestern circuit for a bit by that time, but when Sharon began making her presence obvious I came back here. I moved into an apartment, told people that my husband had died in an automobile accident. I got a Social Security card. I looked pretty good, and I had a good telephone voice. I've been a receptionist ever since."

I looked at her a little dubiously. "Most women with a background like you've described wouldn't find it quite so easy to fit into the straight life."

She lit another cigarette, exhaled. "Nobody ever said it was easy. I did it, that's all."

"You were never tempted to make a little extra money on the side?"

"Tempted? Sure. But I never gave in. I had a job and a daughter. I wanted to keep both of them."

"How about romantic involvements?"

She handed me the folder after a last brief look. "None. Oh, there were advances made to me from time to time, but that's one thing about me that didn't change; I still see men as good for only one thing."

"Let's talk about Sharon, then. What's the story?"

For the first time she looked as if her calm façade might crack, but it was only temporary. Then she was in control again. I wondered if control was something she'd learned while doing her job on Postoffice Street.

"She went out on Friday night. She didn't come home. The next morning I called Dino."

"I've got to admit that's succinct," I said. "So. Where'd she go?"

"I don't know." She blew another of the smoky jets.

"Did she walk? Ride? Go alone, or with someone?"

"I'm not sure."

"Look," I said, feeling exasperated already, "you must know *something*."

She ground out the cigarette, looking at the ashtray instead of me. "No," she finally said. "I *don't* have to know something. My daughter lived here with me, but that doesn't mean we communicated."

Something clicked. "She knew," I said. I thought about it a minute. "She didn't know, and then she knew. Recently."

Evelyn Matthews looked at the folder I was holding, but she still didn't look at me. "Yes," she said.

I thought that now we were getting somewhere and that this might turn out to be easier than I'd thought. "Isn't it possible that she just went away for a while to figure out how she felt about things? She'll probably call soon, or come home. You can see that she's had a shock."

She nodded reluctantly. "It's possible, but I don't believe it."

"Did she have any money? A car?"

"She might have a little money of her own. She's been working part time in a little shop on The Strand."

"What does she do the rest of the time?"

"She goes to the community college. She wants to be a lawyer."

"Boyfriends?"

"No one steady." She reached for the Marlboro pack, picked it up, then set it back down. "I smoke too much," she said. "There's a boy she likes, Terry Shelton. You could talk to him. He works at the shop, too."

"What about the car?"

"I have a car. Sharon doesn't. Mine's in the garage."

It was time to backtrack a little. "How'd you get to know Dino?"

She smiled a reminiscent smile. "He used to hang around

the house. He was just a kid, eight, ten maybe. He and Ray came around sometimes. We all knew he was related to the bosses, so we were nice to him. He never came in at night, just in the afternoon sometimes."

Something must have showed in my face.

"Not nice to him the way you're thinking," she said. "Jesus. He was just a kid."

"Sorry," I said.

She waved it away. "No more than what most people would think. We were whores, after all. But we weren't as bad as all that. Anyway, Dino remembers. He thinks of me as sort of one of the family. There's not many of the old bunch left around here, you know?"

I said I knew. "Did Sharon have any friends at the college, anyone she might have confided in?"

She thought about it for a second or two. "There's one girl there, Julie Gregg, who works in the social studies department. Sharon mentioned her a few times."

"One more thing. How did Sharon find out about your past?"

She reached for another cigarette and lit it, whether she smoked too much or not. "I wish I knew," she said. "I wish I knew."

$\triangledown$

4

THE LAST TIME I saw Jan was about six months before she disappeared. She drove up to Dallas to visit me one weekend. I'd been promising to get down to the island for nearly a year, but I'd never done it. We went out to eat, to a movie, and talked about the old days. She seemed happy and pleased with her life.

When her letters stopped, I got worried, but not worried enough. And by the time I did get worried enough, it was already too late. I hoped that I wouldn't be too late for Sharon. Maybe I was thinking that in some way finding Sharon would make up for losing Jan. Or maybe in some way I hoped that in looking for Sharon I could find a trace of Jan, something new that would put me on the right track. Whatever it was, I'd decided to give it a try. If Dino hadn't convinced me, talking to Evelyn Matthews had. I thought she was an honest woman.

It was still cold when I left her house, but the sky was beginning to clear a little. It was dark, and I could see a star or two, which meant that the front had managed to push its way out into the Gulf and that tomorrow would be considerably warmer. You could never tell about February, though.

I drove back to my house, which really wasn't that far, and parked in the backyard. Nameless materialized at my feet when I stepped out of the car and followed me inside. I made sure his water bowl was full and tore open a packet of Tender Vittles for him. While he was scarfing it down, I went upstairs to check out the refrigerator. There wasn't really anything I could do about Sharon Matthews until the next day, and I was hungry.

The refrigerator still held what it had when I'd looked earlier, half a loaf of bread, part of a jar of peanut butter, a nearly empty two-liter bottle of Big Red, a piece of cheddar cheese wrapped up in plastic wrap so that I could see the greenish mold spots on it, a couple of Hormel wieners, and a dish of something that had probably been edible once, a long time ago. Having had peanut butter for lunch, I decided to spend some of Dino's money and treat myself to a hamburger.

I went back downstairs, carrying a load of laundry. Nameless was chasing a roach the size of one of those thick pink erasers I used in the first grade. I watched until he caught it, then shooed him away and crunched it underfoot before it could run away. He'd weakened it considerably, or I never would have caught it.

I dumped the dirty clothes in the washer, pitched in some Tide, which had been on sale last week, and started the washer. By then Nameless was at the door, ready to go out. He didn't spend any of the nighttime hours in the house, not by choice. He was nothing more than an orange blur moving through the darkness by the time I got to the first step.

Monday night in February—the streets weren't crowded. I drove down Broadway to the golden arches and ate two cheeseburgers and a large order of fries. The fries were better than the burgers.

It was still early, so I went home and tried to read more

of *Absalom, Absalom*. This time I found the going a little easier—which worried me a bit, but not much. I read until ten o'clock; then I went to bed. I was surprised next morning to realize that I had drifted off to sleep almost immediately.

I got up at seven o'clock, ate a piece of dry toast, and let Nameless in. He was ready for more Tender Vittles. There was a little sun, and the temperature was already edging up toward fifty degrees. I got the washing out of the machine and tossed it in the dryer. It was mostly sweatshirts, shorts, and jeans, so leaving it in the washer overnight hadn't hurt it.

I got dressed and drove down to the west end of the seawall for my run. I wanted to get it done early because if it warmed up and the sun came out, there'd be a lot more people on the wall than there had been the day before. Besides, I had work to do.

Back at the house, I took a shower, dressed, and pitched Nameless out. He looked so comfortable balled up on my bed that I hated to do it, but I wasn't sure when I'd be back in. I didn't want to deprive him of his early evening rambles.

The community college campus was over near Ball High School, so the drive wasn't far.

I had a little trouble finding a parking spot. The college had just built a big new library and classroom building on the spot that had once been a parking lot. There was a new lot a couple of blocks away. I parked there and walked back to the campus.

At not quite ten o'clock on a Tuesday morning, most of the students on campus were in class. I stopped one who wasn't, a girl who was carrying a can of Coke down the hall, and she directed me to the political science department. They don't call it "social studies" anymore, the way Evelyn Matthews had. That's high school terminology.

The office wasn't large, and there was a blond girl sitting

at a desk. She didn't look up when I stepped through the open door because she was too busy stapling papers together, after she gathered them from the various neat stacks lined up on the desk. She was muttering something under her breath. It sounded like, "I hate this. Why is this in my life?" I stood there for a second or two waiting for her to notice me, but she was so intent on her gathering and stapling that she never looked up. Finally I tapped on the door frame.

She turned and focused a pair of very large blue eyes on me. "Oh," she said. "I'm sorry. I didn't hear you come in. Can I help you?"

"Looks as if you're the one who needs help," I said.

"Oh, no." She gave an embarrassed laugh and glanced at the papers on the desk. "It's just that we *do* have a collator, but Dr. Samuels always forgets to set the machine correctly. Then he brings his papers down here for me to collate."

She was dressed casually in jeans and a blue shirt, but she certainly had nice eyes.

"You do this for everyone in the department?" I said.

"Not everyone. Mostly just Dr. Samuels." She looked at me questioningly. "Are you looking for Dr. Martin?"

I asked who Dr. Martin was.

"He's the department head. He's in class right now, but he'll be back at ten-fifty."

I stepped a little farther into the office and saw that there was a door connecting this room with another, larger one, presumably Dr. Martin's.

"No," I said. "I'm not looking for Dr. Martin. Actually, I'd like to talk to you, if you're Julie Gregg."

"I'm Julie," she said. "What did you want to talk to me about?"

"It's about Sharon Matthews," I said.

"Sharon? What's the matter with Sharon?"

"Probably nothing. Did you see her here at school yesterday?"

She thought about it. "Well, no. But we don't have any classes together on Monday/Wednesday/Friday. Is she sick?"

"She seems to have left home unexpectedly," I said. "Her mother's worried."

"Her mother," Julie said.

"Anything wrong with her mother?"

"No, nothing," Julie said, looking back at the papers on her desk as if the job of collating and stapling them had suddenly grown incredibly fascinating.

So much for keeping Evelyn's past a deep, dark secret, I thought.

"Sharon told you, huh?" I said.

Julie forced herself to look back at me. "Told me what?"

"Look, Julie, let's not beat around the bush. That might work on an essay quiz in history class, but this is a real live person we're talking about here. Sharon told you about her mother. Did she tell you anything else?"

"Are you from the police?" she asked suddenly.

"No," I said. I got out my billfold and showed her my license.

"I don't have to talk to you, then, do I?"

Kids these days are getting too smart. Must be all that TV they watch.

"Not unless you want me to help Sharon," I said.

"Maybe Sharon doesn't want your help. Maybe you just ought to leave her alone." She reached out and started taking papers off the stacks, one paper off each stack. There was purple printing on each sheet.

"But you don't know, do you?" I said. "Maybe she needs my help."

"I don't think so. I don't think she'd want anyone sent by her mother. Not now. I think she just needs to sort things out. She'll be back in school in a day or so."

She'd managed to convince herself. Her hands picked up speed. The papers slipped easily off one another, and she guided them into a neat stack, tapping the bottoms on the desktop and stapling them together.

"OK," I said. "Maybe I'll talk to you again, later on. If she doesn't come back."

"She'll be back."

Since she had never asked me to sit down, I didn't have to get up. I just walked back out through the office door.

"Maybe," I said over my shoulder as I started back down the hall.

It was well up in the morning now. The clouds were white and the sun was breaking through so often that the weatherman would have to classify the day as partly sunny. The temperature was rising, too, along with the humidity. It was going to be a typical day on the Island.

I got in the Subaru and turned on the radio, tuning in to one of the oldies stations from Houston. It didn't matter which one. Out of the hundreds, maybe thousands, of hits in the 1950s and 1960s, the playlists seem to include only about forty records. You could hear everything the Supremes ever did, but you'd listen forever before anyone ever played "Smoky Places."

This time I got lucky. Roy Orbison. "Running Scared." It almost restored my faith in radio.

I didn't start the car, just sat there in the parking lot listening to the song and wondering how long it would be before someone came along to tell me that I was parked illegally. I didn't have a parking sticker, but I hadn't looked for a spot marked "Visitors."

I thought about Sharon Matthews and her mother. I thought a little bit about Julie Gregg. Every case is different, but I couldn't seem to get a handle on this one. Julie appeared to think that Sharon might have taken off because of what she found out about her mother. I'd had that thought at first myself, and it could still be right. I needed to find out more about what kind of person Sharon was, whether she was accustomed to doing impulsive things like striking out on her own.

I didn't think Julie would be much help. She'd clammed up when she decided that I was too close to Sharon's mother. I wondered what, exactly, Sharon had told Julie, and why. Well, I could always talk to her again. I started the car and drove down to The Strand.

The Strand takes in roughly the area from Postoffice Street to Strand, bounded by Twentieth and Twenty-fifth streets. There are any number of artsy little shops there, selling everything from clothes to antiques to trinkets, most of them expensive. There were a few tourists wandering around even on a Tuesday in February—they seemed to like the restored buildings. The locals tend to avoid the place, as they do the beach, except in December when the Dickens on The Strand festival is held. Some of them even dress in Victorian costume then and parade around the streets. Some of them come to the Mardi Gras celebration in March, too, taking part in the parades and general good times along with the hundreds of thousands of tourists.

During Mardi Gras, there's no possible chance of finding a parking spot, and I've been told that hotel rooms in the area go for nine hundred dollars or so, but today I parked with no trouble at all pretty near the shop I was looking for.

I had to walk up the steps to the sidewalk, which was nearly as high as my shoulder. I could look back and see the *Elissa*, a square-rigged sailing ship, anchored at Pier Twenty-two.

There were really two shops with practically adjoining doors not ten feet from the steps. One of them appeared to deal mostly in soaps, but the other, the one that interested me, had a window display intended to appeal to someone with a little money who was looking for something "different."

There were kaleidoscopes, jars with clever sayings on them ("For Belly Button Lint"), handmade dolls, and even

Christmas decorations. I opened the door and went inside, where there was more of the same, and even a watercolor portrait of Dolly Parton, fully life size. There were tables with dolls on them, small rocking chairs with teddy bears sitting in them, and shelves loaded with mirrors and ceramic boxes and cloisonné thimbles. To the right there was a glass candy counter with a cash register sitting on top of it. The place smelled of potpourri.

But there was no one in the shop but me.

I threaded my way around the tables and chairs to another room located to the back of the shop. There were more shelves, covered with coffee cups that had handles shaped like alligators. There were lamps made from sea urchins.

But there was no one there, either.

I made my way back to the cash register. The shop couldn't run itself. Maybe Terry Shelton, if he was working that day, had gone out for coffee. Maybe he would be back in a minute.

I waited.

No one came. I looked out the front window. There was no tourist traffic on the sidewalk. I waited some more. Still no one.

After nearly fifteen minutes, I decided to go next door. The place was filled with soap of every description, or at least every odor. As soon as I opened the door, I was almost overpowered.

The soap covered the shelves and the counters. It was in baskets and boxes. It was wrapped and unwrapped. I had a sudden urge to go home and take a shower.

There was someone behind the counter, and I wouldn't have minded if she'd come home and shared the shower with me. She was about twenty-six or -seven, tall, with an aristocratic face and nose. I'm a sucker for an aristocratic nose. She had on a pink warm-up suit that matched the wrappings of most of the soap.

I walked over to the counter. "Business seems pretty slow," I said. I'm never at a loss for a conversational gambit.

She didn't seem to mind my lack of snappy patter. She was probably bored by the inactivity.

"It'll probably pick up in the afternoon," she said. "It usually does." She had an alto voice that did strange things to the base of my spine. I fantasized briefly about Humphrey Bogart and Dorothy Malone in the bookstore scene in *The Big Sleep*.

"Seen many people going in next door?" I said.

"Not many. I saw you, though."

"I couldn't find anyone to help me. There's no one at the cash register."

She leaned forward, resting her elbows on the counter. "You wanted to buy that portrait of Dolly Parton, right?"

"Not really. Now if it were painted on black velvet, I might be interested."

She laughed. It was deep and throaty, not aristocratic at all. "To match the one you have of Elvis?"

"No, of John Wayne."

She looked at me, really looked at me, for the first time. I found myself wishing that she wore glasses, so that she could take them off like Dorothy Malone had done.

"I'd have guessed that you were more of the Clint Eastwood type," she said. "You do kind of squint, you know."

"Comes from too much time in the sun."

"You're no beach bum, though."

"Not exactly. I'm more of a generalized kind of a bum."

"And you really aren't interested in Dolly Parton?"

"Well . . ."

"Her picture, I mean."

"To tell the truth, no."

"I don't suppose that I could sell you a bar of soap, either."

"I don't object to smelling good," I said. "But I wouldn't want you to think I'm a sissy."

"I don't think you'd have to worry about that." She smiled. "So. What did you want next door?"

"I wanted to talk to a kid named Terry Shelton. But like I said, there's no one there."

She thought about that. "That's strange. I mean, we aren't exactly in a rush hour here, but no one would go off and leave the shop wide open. Not even Terry."

"You know him?"

"I know him a little. From being around here."

"What's he like?"

She stood up, taking her elbows off the counter. Then she walked around to stand beside me. "He's, well, flaky. A little weird. But nice. Are you sure nobody's in there?" She peered out the door as if she might be able to see inside the other shop.

"I wouldn't bet my life that he wasn't, but I stood in there for nearly fifteen minutes and never saw anyone."

She walked to the door. I followed her. There were no tourists on our side of the street, though we could see people walking up on Mechanic Street at the crossing a block away.

"Should we do something?" she said.

I'd been wondering the same thing, but I wasn't sure what we could do.

"Maybe we should go over there and look," she said. "He might've had a heart attack or something."

"How old is he?"

"Old?"

"I've never met him," I said, "but I was under the impression that he was a little young to be a heart attack risk."

"Oh. I guess you're right. He's younger than I am, I'm sure."

I refrained from asking how old that might be.

"Let's go over there and check," she said.

"OK," I said. I didn't have anything better to do, though I didn't think we'd find anything I hadn't already seen.

We went out the door of the soap shop and in the door of the shop where there was no one at home.

"See?" I said. "Not a soul around."

She glanced over the shop. "There's another room."

"I've been in there. Nobody there, either."

I walked over to the cash register. In keeping with the shop, it was not one of the new electronic models, but an old cast-iron one. You had to know how to make change yourself to operate one of those babies.

"What did you mean about Terry being weird?" I asked.

"Well, I don't know exactly. He's always talking about those heavy metal groups. You know. Metallica. Whitesnake."

"And that's weird?"

"Not really, I guess, but for someone his age it sort of is. I mean, most guys grow out of that stuff by the time they get out of high school, but not Terry. He goes to all the concerts, buys the T-shirts and wears them to work, plays their music all the time." She looked around the shop. "I knew something was wrong. I don't hear the music. He's not supposed to play it loud; the owner gets upset. But it's always on so you can hear it."

"I don't even see a radio," I said.

She pointed to a grille set in the wall over a shelf in the back of the shop. It was only then that I noticed that the shelf disguised a door set in the wall.

"There's a radio in the storeroom," she said.

"I'll check it out," I said. "You wait here in case a shopper comes in." I wasn't sure that I'd find anything, but I thought it might be better to look alone.

It was just as well that I did. I opened the door, swinging the shelf out with it. There was no light on in the storeroom, but I could see that the walls were lined with rough shelving that was covered with cardboard boxes of various sizes. I could also see, in the light spilling in from the room where

I stood, a pair of white leather Reeboks on the floor. The shoes were on feet, which were attached to legs. I opened the door farther. There was someone lying on the floor of the storeroom. He was lying facedown, so I couldn't see what he looked like. On the back of his T-shirt were the words IF IT'S TOO LOUD YOU'RE TOO OLD in red letters outlined in gold.

I had a feeling that I'd found Terry Shelton.

5

THE GIRL FROM THE soap shop, whose name I learned was Vicky Bryan, called the police, who questioned us separately. I'd dealt with the Galveston police before, when I was looking for Jan, but I didn't know the one who was grilling me, a detective named Gerald Barnes. I didn't feel any particular obligation to tell him I'd been looking for Shelton. I just said that I'd been in the shop, noticed that no one was around, and gone next door to see if the girl inside knew what was going on.

It was a mistake.

What can I say? I was rusty. I hadn't been into a serious investigation for quite some time. I should have realized that Vicky would remember I'd been asking questions about Shelton and that she would see no reason not to mention that fact.

Barnes was mildly chapped. "You're trying to dick me around," he said after returning from a consultation with the cop who'd been talking to Vicky. "I really don't like to be dicked around. It's boring, and it's a waste of time."

Barnes was not an imposing man. In fact, he was somewhat slight, and he wore glasses. He looked more like a computer programmer than a cop. But the implied threat in his voice was real enough, and I figured he could back it up. He could get help if he needed it, and I couldn't.

"Look," I said. "I'll level with you." I gave a look at my license. "You don't know me, but some of the members of your department do." I told him why I'd come back to the Island. "You can check me out with Ben Dancer. I've talked to him about Jan." I was pretty sure Dancer would give me a clean bill of health.

"So what were you doing here?" Barnes said.

"I'd heard from someone that the kid working here might have known Jan. When I didn't see anyone, I asked next door. The girl there thought we should check things out, and we found the body. You think I wanted anything to do with a murder? No way. All I wanted was out. The girl didn't know my name. I could have skipped, but I told her to call you while I stayed here. You can ask her. Anyway, I've got my own problems, and I don't want anything to do with this one."

Barnes gave me a speculative look through his black-rimmed glasses and brushed his thin brown hair off his forehead. "You think this had anything to do with your sister?"

"No," I said. "It's been too long since she disappeared. It would be too much of a coincidence."

He thought about it. "And you know Dancer?" he said.

"Sure. He tried to help me out. He's a good man, but there was nothing he could do."

"All right," Barnes said. "I'll talk to him. What's your local address?"

I gave it to him, along with the phone number. "You need me, you get in touch," I said. "I'll be glad to help out."

He put the notebook back in his pocket. He didn't look happy with me, but he knew where to find me if Dancer let me down.

I got out of there.

* * *

I wanted to talk to Vicky some more. I thought she might know more than I'd been able to find out so far, but I had to talk to Dino first. This was turning out to be a little more complicated, not to mention dangerous, than I'd expected.

Terry Shelton had been killed by someone strong. I didn't have time to look at him very long, but there was hardly a mark on him. My guess was that his neck had been broken. I hadn't searched his body, but I'd looked around the cash register and found a package of Camel filters with a matchbook stuck down in the cellophane. I'd slipped the package into my pocket. How was Barnes to know I didn't smoke? The matchbook was from a Houston club called The Sidepocket. It was the only clue I had, if it was a clue.

Barnes had kept at me for a long time, so it was well after the lunch hour. I wanted to eat before I talked to Dino, and Shrimp and Stuff was on the way home. I pulled the car in behind the building and parked. Shrimp and Stuff doesn't pretend to be fancy, but the food is cheap and good.

I opened the door of the restaurant and stepped in, glancing at the menu hanging from the fourteen-foot ceiling over the cash register. The menu items were painted on two pieces of wood, brown on white, but the prices were inked on poster board and stuck beside the menu names, just in case another oil spill came along and drove up the price of seafood. It had warmed up enough outside so that the ceiling fans had been turned on; the blades revolved slowly over the few tables in the place. I stepped up to the register and ordered a shrimp and crab po-boy, told the cashier my initials, and sat down to wait.

When my initials were called out, I went up to the counter and got my sandwich. There were only a couple of other late diners, and I hardly glanced at them. My mind was on Terry Shelton and Sharon Matthews, for whom things didn't look too good right then. Obviously her disappearance was more than just a runaway. If it involved murder, as it appeared to do, it was getting beyond my area of expertise. I could find people, or I used to be able to, but murder was another thing entirely.

To make matters worse, I'd already lied to the cops about my interest in the case. If they ran into me again, they weren't going to be pleased. And that was understating the case. I had the idea that if I gave Barnes half a chance, he would charge me with everything but mopery and stash me so far back in one of the TDC's correctional units that I'd never see the Gulf of Mexico again. Some people just don't like private eyes, especially private eyes that lie to them. And who could blame them?

I finished my sandwich, gathered up my Styrofoam plate and the crumpled napkins, and threw them all in a large brown trashcan. A handprinted sign attached to a railing behind the can said SAVE ALL BEER BOTTLES. I wasn't sure whether it was a command or request, but I didn't have a beer bottle anyway, so I went on out.

I drove over to Dino's tan-colored Georgian house, stopped the car, and got out. Ray answered the door. I was beginning to expect him to be dressed in livery, but he was wearing a brown suit that clearly had no unnatural fibers in its composition, a crisp white cotton shirt, a silk tie with a sort of paisley pattern, and brown shoes. Probably Stacy-Adams. I could never figure anyone who would wear a suit in the middle of the day, but maybe if I'd looked a little more like Ray, Julie Gregg would've talked more to me.

"You admiring my outfit or trying to remember your sales pitch?" Ray said.

"I need to talk to Dino," I said. "It's important."

"It better be. He's in the middle of *Days of Our Lives*. You know, 'Like sands through the hourglass . . .' "

I said I didn't know.

"Well, you better come on in anyway."

He led me into the living room, where Dino sat on his couch watching the television set. He was crouched slightly forward, holding the remote control device in his left hand. He was wearing a Hawaiian shirt and a pair of blue slacks, much more casual than Ray, though still not in my class. Ray and I stood respectfully silent until a commercial for a feminine hygiene product came on.

"Those damn ads always embarrass me," Dino said, which I thought was a strange remark for a man whose entire personal fortune—which was no doubt considerable—was based on the income of a huge gambling and prostitution operation. He turned the television's sound down and looked at me. "What's happening?"

"I hate to interrupt your program."

"That's OK. Hasn't been worth a damn in years, not since Doug and Julie left. Julie's back now, but it's not the same. Amanda left too. She's on that *Newhart* show. You ever catch that one?"

I shook my head. "Afraid not."

"Well, it's too late anyway. It's off the air now. But it was pretty good. The last show was a classic."

I said I was sorry I'd missed it.

"Yeah, you should've seen it, all right. You remember how they had this thing on *Dallas* a few years back, about how Bobby's death was all just a dream? It was a takeoff on that."

I had to admit that I didn't even know who Bobby was.

"I guess you didn't come here to talk about TV shows, did you?" Dino glanced back over at his set, where the soap opera had resumed. He didn't turn the sound up, though. "Sit down. Ray'll bring us something to drink. I guess you want a Big Red."

"That'll be fine."

Ray took his cue and disappeared. I went over and sat in the same chair I'd occupied the day before.

"Don't tell me you found the girl already," Dino said.

"Don't worry. I won't."

Dino sneaked a look at the TV screen. "What, then? It must be something, or you wouldn't be back so soon. You haven't spent that thousand already, have you?"

"No," I said. "Not yet."

"So? Gimme a clue. You're the detective, not me."

I told him that I'd talked to Evelyn Matthews, found out about Sharon's friends, and visited Julie Gregg. By then Ray had come back with the drinks. I took a swallow of Big Red.

"I went to see another friend of Sharon's today," I said. "He worked down on The Strand. Name was Terry Shelton."

I was watching Dino closely, but he didn't seem to notice the use of the past tense. Ray had retired back out of my line of sight, so I couldn't see how he'd reacted, if he'd reacted at all.

"So what did this Shelton have to say?" Dino asked.

"Very little. He was dead when I got there."

Dino carefully set his glass on the curved-leg coffee table. "Dead?"

"That's right. Dead."

"The police know about this?"

"They know. There was a witness with me when I found the body, though, so I'm not in any trouble."

"Who's this witness?" He picked up the glass again and took a drink.

"No one important. The girl who works in the shop next door to where I found Shelton."

"What did you tell the cops?"

"Nothing much. I didn't mention Sharon Matthews. I gave them a line about Jan. I wasn't sure how much you wanted them to know."

"There was a time when we could trust the cops on the Island," Dino said. "But not now."

I took that to mean that his family pretty much had the cops in their pockets back in the 1930s and 1940s. Well, it was true, or so everyone said. But times had changed. Dino had the money, but not the power.

"The problem," I said, "is that this isn't just about some little girl who's run away from home, not anymore. This is a whole lot worse, and I'm not sure I want to have anything to do with it."

Dino looked hurt. "You trying to jack up your price, Tru?"

"You know me better than that."

"Yeah, I guess I do. How's the knee today?"

"Enough with the knee. It's not the knee."

"I know that. I know that. It's just that this bothers me. Even in the old days, I never heard my uncles talk about murder."

He was telling the truth, I was sure. His uncles might have controlled the Island, and they might have been heavily into enterprises that some people might narrow-mindedly have called criminal, but murder was a different story. The uncles were never mixed up in murder.

Dino sighed, touched a button on his remote, and caused the TV screen to darken. He was going to have to deal with real life, whether he liked it or not. He looked over my shoulder. "What d'you think, Ray?"

"Sounds like maybe someone else is looking for the kid," he said. "How'd this Shelton guy die?"

"I don't know," I said. "I didn't see any marks on him. No blood. His head was at a pretty funny angle. Looked as if maybe his neck was broken."

"Damn," Dino said. "So where does this leave us?"

"There are a couple of people I could talk to again," I said. "And there's one other thing. But the real question is, am I going on with this?"

"Why not?" Dino said.

"I told you," I said. "It's not a missing person thing now. It's murder."

"You want out, huh? You wanta quit?"

"I'm not sure what I want. I think about Jan, and I know that murder wouldn't stop me in that case. I guess what I want is for you to say you didn't have anything to do with this Shelton mess. That you had no idea there was anything like that involved."

"How long have we known each other?" Dino said. "Forever, right?"

"I guess," I said.

"No guessing. Ball High? Knocking heads in football practice? Chasing the same girls? Forever."

"OK," I said. "Forever."

"Ray too."

Ray hadn't been in high school with us, though the Island would have integrated fairly willingly. He'd been around, though. Even then he and Dino were close.

"Yeah," I said. "Ray too."

"So I'm telling you we didn't know. No shit, now. Right, Ray?"

"Right," Ray said.

"We don't know any more about murder than you do," Dino said. "Think how Evelyn's gonna feel when she finds out about this. Did you tell her yet?"

"No," I said. "I thought I'd better leave that to you."

"Right. I'll call her. You gonna stick with this?"

"All right," I said. I had a feeling I was making a big mistake, but I didn't have anything better to do. The house painting business was lousy. And I'd known Dino forever. If I couldn't trust him, who could I trust?

"Great. You need anything, you let me know. But don't get in trouble with the cops. I know a few of them, but I can't help you very much there."

"There's one thing you can help me with. The other thing I mentioned." I took out the cigarette pack and slipped out the matchbook. "You can tell me about this place." I handed the matchbook to him.

He looked at it for a minute, not saying anything, then tossed it across the room to Ray. "See what you can find out," he said.

Ray went out with the matchbook. "I still have a few contacts for that kind of stuff," Dino said. He drained his glass and set it on the table. I still had half of my Big Red left.

"Where'd you get the matchbook?" he asked.

"From Terry Shelton, I think. Before the cops came."

Dino grinned. He had big, square teeth, like tombstones. "He wanted you to have it, right?"

"Something like that," I said.

"I hope the cops don't find out you lifted it."

"I hope you're not planning to tell them."

He grinned again but didn't say anything. He and his uncles would have gotten along pretty well, I think, had their business still been thriving and he been a part of it. As far as I knew, he was a clean, upright citizen, but he had the makings of a first-rate criminal.

Ray came back into the room on little cat feet. I felt that he was there, but I didn't hear him return. I turned to look, and there he was.

"You saw the address on the matchbook?" he said.

"Somewhere on Telephone Road. I don't remember the number."

"You been down Telephone lately?" Dino asked.

I turned back to him. "Not lately. It's part of Highway 35, isn't it? Comes into Houston from Pearland and runs under the Gulf Freeway?"

"That's right," Dino said. "From the numbers on that matchbook, I'd guess The Sidepocket isn't in one of the classier areas of town. What about it Ray?"

"You'd be guessing right."

Although I hadn't been in that part of Houston recently, I recalled that there were parts of Telephone Road, after you passed Hobby Airport and got closer to the part of Interstate

45, that Houstonians call the Gulf Freeway, where there were some fairly sleazy areas. You'd find motels that hadn't been painted in years, with gravel drives and signs offering rooms by the hour, and probably a few clubs like The Sidepocket.

"Who owns it?" Dino asked.

"Somebody named Ferguson runs the place. I wouldn't say for sure that he owns it. It's one of those places that has a lot of struggling local bands playing there because they're cheap. Goes for the chains and leather crowd. I took the liberty of asking the friend I called to tip the word to Ferguson that Tru might be dropping in this afternoon late for a chat. I didn't say why, but I made it out to be a favor to us."

"You going up there?" Dino asked.

"I might as well."

There were other things I would rather have done, but if Terry Shelton was tied to Sharon Matthews, The Sidepocket was as good a place as any to start. Maybe Sharon had been there with Terry, and maybe someone had seen her. You never knew where something might lead you in one of these cases.

I had put my glass down on the floor, and I bent down to pick it up and drink what was left of the Big Red. "Are you interested at all in who killed this Shelton, if his murder doesn't have anything to do with Sharon?"

I didn't think that Dino was going in for humanitarianism these days, and I was right. "No," he said. "Unless it involves Sharon, stay out of it completely. If you can find out something about her at the club, fine. If you can't, drop it."

"Suits me," I said. I wasn't going in for humanitarianism, either. I hoped that I could just forget all about Shelton and that his death was a side issue, but I wasn't counting on it. "How about my matchbook?"

Ray tossed it to me, and I grabbed it out of the air. I slipped it back in my pocket with the package of cigarettes. Then I stood up. "I guess I'll be going."

"You going to be doing any dancing at this club?" Dino asked, glancing at my knee.

"Depends on the band."

"OK," he said. "Ray'll let you out."

By the time I was out of the room, I heard the TV set come to life again.

6

I WANTED TO GO by the house to check on Nameless and have a quick sandwich before my trip into Houston, and as I drove I thought about Dino. It was hard to believe that his whole life now was bounded by a television screen, but I supposed it was possible. He had all the money he would ever need, and he could keep up his old contacts by telephone. It seemed that he had no desire to enter the world his uncles had been so fond of and found so profitable.

Of course, at the end of things, his uncles hadn't found their world to be such an ideal one. Hundreds, if not thousands, of slot machines littered the bottom of Galveston Bay, the big clubs were closed forever, and the Hollywood stars didn't come to the Island anymore. Neither, for that matter, did the Houston high rollers, and many BOIs traced the decline of the Island's economy to that ill-fated day when a certain Texas attorney general thought he might get elected governor if he could clean up the most notable den of iniquity. That he was completely and absolutely wrong, that most people both on the Island and elsewhere actually resented what he did, came as a huge surprise to him, though not to anyone else in the state.

Galveston had tried recently to vote gambling's legal return to the Island, but the referendum had failed. The churches, of course, were strongly opposed, and some of the rich and powerful, such of them as were left, thought that gambling would be bad for the city's newly created image of historical browsing ground. There were, however, two cruise ships that took happy gamblers out beyond the twelve-mile limit every weekend to relieve them of some of their money at the blackjack tables, the poker tables, the slots.

I didn't know what Dino thought about all of this. He'd been a roistering youth, but apparently all that kind of thing was behind him now.

And Ray seemed quite content to pass his time sticking by Dino in a weird sort of Old Family Retainer way. Maybe it was his way of repaying the uncles, who'd after all pulled him literally out of the whorehouse. It's possible that for the merest second a suspicion of the nature of Ray's relationship with Dino may have crossed my mind, but if it did I dismissed it instantly. I'd known both of them too well and too long to think that they were gay; they certainly hadn't been when they were younger.

I pulled up in back of the house and just managed to get out of the car before Nameless zipped up to the steps in an orange streak. I guess he wanted another package of cat food, which I promptly doled out to him. He began purring as soon as he stuck his nose in the bowl. I wasn't sure how it was possible for a cat to purr and eat at the same time, but it was a trick that Nameless managed with easy regularity.

I went on up to the second floor, leaving the door open in case Nameless wanted to pay me a visit. It was up to him.

It was time for me to outfit myself for the trip to The Sidepocket. I'm not a member of the heavy metal crowd, or any crowd at all for that matter. I have several different outfits that I once wore to visit various kinds of night spots, but I didn't think any of them would be appropriate for The Sidepocket.

For a country and western club, I could have worn my kicker outfit, complete with boots, starched blue Levi's, and white shirt. For a singles bar, I had a very nice natural fiber double-breasted suit in which, if I'd had a haircut lately, which I hadn't, I could pass for a rising executive. Not a young executive, but an executive nevertheless. But for the heavy metal crew, I'd just have to get by with my usual sweatshirt and faded jeans. At my age, I was going to look out of place anyway.

While I was eating cold bread spread with cold peanut butter, Nameless deigned to come up and poke his head in the door. What he saw was of so little interest to him that he turned almost immediately and went back down, his tail held high. It was a fairly attractive tail, if you liked cats' tails, with dark orange rings around the lighter orange fur that covered it. He was too polite to sit at the downstairs door and howl, so I went to let him out.

After the sandwich I had a couple of swallows of nearly flat Big Red from the two-liter bottle and left the rest, probably another two swallows, for when I came home. I watched the news on one of the Houston channels, and the anchorwoman told me that times were steadily getting better for the Gulf Coast area. The media had been saying that at least once a month for the last two years, though I hadn't noticed any real improvement. I didn't know why they kept repeating it unless they hoped that saying it would make it so.

After the news report I went downstairs, got in the Subaru, and headed for the Gulf Freeway.

Broadway actually runs right into the freeway, or becomes the freeway, whichever you prefer. By the time you pass the Island's only shopping mall, you're pretty well aware that you aren't on a city street any longer. Cars are speeding along in three or four lanes, and you're headed for the tall bridge with its truly superfluous MINIMUM SPEED 40 MPH sign.

Anyone driving forty miles per hour on a Texas highway is taking his life in his hands. In spite of the fact that fifty-five is the maximum you can drive on that part of the Interstate, most drivers figure they can get by with sixty-five, which can easily be upped to seventy-five if they think no one is watching. And most of the drivers on the Gulf Freeway seem thoroughly convinced that no one is watching.

All of this makes life pretty tough if you're the driver of a '79 Subaru. I mashed the accelerator to the floor and tried to keep up with the traffic flow, hoping that no one in a monstrous old Pontiac or Buick from the early 1980s would flatten me without noticing.

At the top of the bridge I glanced over to my right, as I almost always do, at the dark hulk of the old drawbridge. I can recall having waited for what seemed like hours for it to be lowered when I was coming back home from some trip with my family when I was a kid.

It was full dark by now, and farther off to the right the oil refineries and petrochemical plants of Texas City lit up the night like the set of the most expensive science fiction movie ever filmed. The industry wasn't what it had once been, however. It had not been so very long ago that a lot of Texans were driving cars with bumper stickers that said DRIVE 75, FREEZE A YANKEE," but now you were more likely to see something like JUST GIVE US ONE MORE OIL BOOM, LORD. WE PROMISE WE WON'T PISS IT AWAY THIS TIME.

The Gulf Freeway, perennially under construction in one part or another, runs straight as an arrow from Galveston into Houston. Past La Marque, past Texas City, past Dickinson (a place that was once as wide-open as Galveston had been), past League City. You can see their lights if you watch and don't drive too fast. At night the lanes of the freeway seem to be a solid streak of red in front of you, with a solid streak of white headlights coming at you from the other direction. I've often wondered where all those people are going, and it's the same at any hour of the day or night. Maybe tonight they were all heading to one version or another of The Sidepocket. Or maybe they were all just going home. I suppose anything is possible.

I'd traveled the freeway a lot, stopping in all the little towns along the way, when I was looking for Jan. I hadn't found a trace of her in any of them.

When I started seeing the first shopping malls, the traffic increased, if that was possible, but I was still a long way from downtown Houston. After I passed the turnoff to NASA at Webster, I counted four malls before I came to the Telephone Road exit.

I slowed for the exit, turned back to the left under the freeway, and started looking for addresses. Hardly any were posted, but The Sidepocket turned out to be easy to find. It was practically next door to one of the ten-dollar-an-hour motels with FREE IN-ROOM MOVIES. The sign did not add my favorite line from the ads I'd read in the men's magazines when I was a kid: "The kind men like!" They might as well have added it, though. I had a feeling they wouldn't be showing *Bambi*.

The Sidepocket was a rambling building with about a fifty-foot front. Half of it was one story, but on the other half there was an additional level with what might have been an office, or living quarters, or both. The building was painted a medium pink, and the roof was green. Or at least that's the way it looked in the light from the parking lot, what little light there was. Near the only entrance there was an enormous eight-ball painted on the wall. Peering over the ball was a strange-looking individual who appeared to be gripping the ball and hanging his nose over the top like Kilroy. Only his hands, eyes, nose, and spiky black hair were visible. The eyes were wide and staring.

In front of the parking lot was that bane of the Gulf Coast, the portable sign. No one seems to care that every little wind blows the things all over town, smashing into cars, heads, and show windows. This one was lit up from the inside, a bright yellow with black letters stating that tonight's band was AMYL NITRATE AND THE WHIPPETS.

I could see that I was in for a real treat. I could also see that the extension cord from the sign ran right across the white gravel parking lot to an outlet on the wall of the building. I wondered how frayed the cord would get from the cars driving over it and what would happen in a good rainstorm, or if someone picked it up to move it. Oh, well. It wasn't my sign.

For a Tuesday night, the crowd wasn't bad. There were quite a few cars in the parking lot, and while there weren't any BMWs, there weren't any '62 Falcons, either. And only one '79 Subaru.

I parked as close to the building as I could get and stepped out of the car. The walls weren't vibrating, exactly, but I swear I could feel the vibrations in the ground through the soles of my Nikes. It was only then that I thought of earplugs, and by then it was much too late. I told myself that I was a tough P.I. on a case and that earplugs were for wimps. I didn't convince myself, but I went on inside.

The lighting was dim, but not too bad. I could see all I wanted to see. Amyl and the boys were on stage, flanked by amplifiers the size of the car I had just parked. There were two guitars, a bass, a drummer, and someone on keyboards. The lead singer, or screamer, was at the microphone yelling something about poison and death. He was wearing a leather vest, ripped jeans, and a survival knife strapped to his right calf. Except for his head, which was covered with very long black hair, he was hairless as a snake and just about as skinny. He had the bass. The other members of the band were just as fashionably dressed, and all of them sported tattoos—skulls, dragons, tigers—that sort of thing.

I forced my way through the wall of sound up to the bar.

The bartender looked at me, and I pointed to the Lone Star sign at his back. He went away and came back with a bottle of beer and a glass. I didn't need the glass.

I took a swallow of beer from the bottle and turned to look around. I drink beer only when I can't get Big Red, and the taste didn't improve my outlook. The crowd was about half punkers and half headbangers. I felt momentarily disoriented, as if I'd wandered onto the set of some B-grade rip-off of the Mad Max movies. One of the punks had hair that looked like Tina Turner's might, if Tina had stuck her finger in a light socket. Another had nothing but five pink spikes running down the middle of his skull.

I looked around a little more. It wasn't easy to see because I could almost feel my eyeballs being pushed back into their sockets by the sonic force of the music that was blasting at me from the stage. It was almost as if the bass player were strumming my right and left ventricles along with the strings of his guitar.

The headbangers went in for spandex tank tops and heavy leather wristbands studded with metal. They also wore fingerless gloves with even more metal studs. Many of them wore thick leather belts that seemed to be strictly decorative, since they didn't fit through any visible loops. Some of the belts held what looked like M-1 cartridges, and some had dangling loops of brass. One woman had on an outfit that was made entirely of small metal spangles, most of them smaller than a dime. She was wearing black boots that came almost to her knees and had a skull blazoned on the fronts. Nearly everyone had tattoos.

Everyone was a lot younger than I was, and I looked very much out of place in my sweatshirt and jeans, but no one seemed to mind.

Amyl and the gang finished up in a frenzy of reverb and feedback. When the music stopped, it was several seconds before I could hear anything at all. Then the dull rumble of conversation, the click of beer bottles, and the scraping of chairs became audible, even though there was still a distant roaring in my ears.

I didn't see anyone who looked like the owner, so I continued to survey the crowd. I was looking for the narc. I figured that in any place like this there were lots of funny-smelling cigarettes to be smoked, and maybe even a line or two of Bolivian happy dust to be inhaled. Therefore there would be an undercover cop in every now and then just in case any of the boys or girls got together enough money to make a really heavy buy.

Of course the heavy buy would never take place because by the time he walked in from the door to a seat, everyone in the place would have the narc spotted for exactly what he was. It's a knack these people have.

I didn't have the knack, though, it not being really necessary to my survival, but it still didn't take me too long at that. He was sitting at a table with a girl in electric blue spandex, the tank top scarcely concealing her generous breasts. I was afraid that if she stood up and shook, the shimmer would blind half the patrons despite the low level of light in the club.

I made my way over to the table, carrying my half-full beer bottle. "Mind if I join you?" I said.

The guy didn't look too happy, but he growled what I took to be an affirmative answer. I hooked an empty chair with my foot, pulled it out, and sat.

If anyone asked me, I couldn't really explain how I knew he was a cop. The hairstyle was a little too studied, maybe, the clothes a little too carefully cared for, the eyes a little too secretive and hard.

"Great band, huh?" I said.

"Damn straight," the girl said. She was drinking Lone Star, too, out of a bottle. She took a pull and set it down solidly on the table to emphasize her remark. The cop didn't say anything.

Over on the bandstand, the lead singer was announcing that it was time for the band to take a break. That was a break for me, too, since I would be able to hear what the two at the table had to tell me.

If they told me anything at all.

We sat there for a few seconds, looking at one another. "I was wondering if maybe you two could do me a favor," I said. If the cop had come there often, he might have seen Sharon Matthews, or Terry, and he might come closer than anyone else in the place to admitting it.

"Maybe," he said. He sounded like he might have gravel in his throat.

I took the picture of Sharon out of my back pocket and slipped it onto the table. It was no longer in its folder. "Ever seen this girl?"

The girl's eyes flickered, but the cop's didn't.

Another few seconds of silence passed. "Well?" I said.

"Maybe," the cop said.

I took out my billfold and, trying not to let everyone in the place see what I was doing, showed him my license.

"She's been in here a few times," the cop said. The girl in the spandex nodded agreement.

"She come in with anybody in particular?" I put my billfold away and slipped the photo off the table.

"Some guy. Harry? Terry?"

"That's the one. They have any friends?"

"Look," the cop said. "I can't afford to say too much."

"There's not a soul in here who doesn't know you work for the city," I said. "You aren't going to sully your reputation."

The girl smiled and leaned back in her chair. The spandex shimmered.

"You're probably right," the cop said. "But that doesn't mean I'm going to just give up the game for you." His eyes were as gray as oysters on the half shell.

"The girl's been missing for three days," I said. "I'm just

trying to make a buck and find her. Her mother's worried."
I decided not to mention what had happened to Terry. I
didn't even like to think about it.

"Give the guy a break, Stan," the girl said. Obviously I
had charmed her.

"All right," Stan said, but I could see he wasn't too happy
about it. "The kid's been in here a few times, like I said.
With this Terry. They don't seem to have too many friends,
mostly sit by themselves. But every now and then they talk
to Chuck. He'd sit with them sometimes."

"Chuck?"

"Ferguson," the girl said. "Chuck Ferguson. He owns the
place."

7

I THANKED THEM FOR the information and got up, leaving the rest of my beer. Then I went over to the bar and asked the bartender where I could find Ferguson.

"Who's looking?" he said.

"Truman Smith," I said. "He's probably expecting me."

"Yeah, he got a call. See that door?" He pointed to a door near the bandstand. I noticed that Amyl Nitrate and the Whippets were picking up their instruments and getting ready for another set.

"I see it," I said.

"Goes up to the second floor. There's a hall. Office is the first door on the right."

"Thanks," I said. I was eager to get up there before the band got cranked up again. I wasn't sure my eardrums were up to it.

I walked down to the door and went on through. There was a narrow wooden stairway, and I followed it up. The hall was paneled with rough plywood. No one was much interested in putting up a front here. I tapped on the first door on my right.

"It's not locked," someone called, so I went on in.

The room was small, about ten by ten. There was a run-down gray couch that looked even worse than mine, a wooden chair, and an old desk that was covered in layers of black varnish.

The man sitting at the desk stood up. He was at least six inches taller than I was, maybe six six or seven, and around fifty-five years old. He was thin, like an aging basketball player. He wore glasses, and his hair was completely white, what there was of it. It was fairly thick on the sides and back, but there were only a few strands combed across the top. He had a white beard as well. Quite a change from the crowd downstairs. He was wearing a white western shirt with pearlized buttons and a pair of brown double knit jeans. He would have looked more at home at Willie Nelson's new place across town than here.

Below us the band was hammering out a song. The floor began to jiggle slightly.

Ferguson stuck out his hand, and I shook it. "Truman Smith," I said.

"Chuck Ferguson. I heard you might be by, but I was expecting you a little earlier."

"I got tied up."

"Doesn't matter. Have a seat." He sat back down in his desk chair. I sat on the couch and immediately sank down about a foot and a half.

"Not much support," I said, struggling to keep myself from disappearing completely from view.

"Chair's more comfortable, even if it doesn't look it," Ferguson said.

I fought my way clear of the couch and sat in the chair. He was right. I took the photo of Sharon Matthews out of my pocket and passed it over to him. "Ever seen her around here?"

He looked at the picture carefully, as if he were trying to memorize every feature of the girl's face. "Could be," he said. "I'm not really sure."

Well, well, I thought. "She was probably with a boy," I said. "Terry Shelton."

He held the picture between his thumb and forefinger and tapped it against his knee. "Shelton. Shelton. Can't say it rings a bell."

"You'd notice them for sure," I said. "They don't look like your regular customers down there." I could feel the vibrations from the bass working their way through the floor, into my legs, and into my heartbeat again.

"You can't tell by the way they look down there," Ferguson said. "Why, some of those people are probably car salesmen. Insurance peddlers. Postmen. Housewives. Most of those tattoos wash off, the hair combs out, the clothes change. You'd be surprised."

I said that I probably would. A particularly thunderous bass line rippled up the walls from below.

"Great little band, isn't it?" Ferguson said. "Those kids are destined for big things."

"I can tell," I said. "You own this place?"

"Sure do. Lock, stock, and rain barrel."

"You should do something about that extension cord running across the parking lot," I said. I reached and took the photo from between his thumb and finger. "Sure you've never seen her before?"

"If I did, she didn't look like that. What's your interest, anyway?"

"She's missing. Her mother hired me to find her."

"That was her mother who called saying you'd be around to see me?"

"That was a friend of the family."

He nodded. "Uh-huh."

I stood up. "Well," I said, "thanks for your time and for taking a look. I heard she'd been in here a time or two. Just thought I'd better check it out."

Ferguson stood, too, sticking out his hand again. Everyone

in Texas likes to shake hands. I shook.

"Sorry I couldn't help you more," he said.

"Just one stop on a long road," I said. "I'll find her sooner or later." *Unless she's like Jan*, I thought. *Jan. Without a trace.*

"Good luck, then," he said, easing me toward the door.

"See you," I said as I left.

"Sure."

The door closed behind me.

The fact that Ferguson was lying didn't especially bother me. I'd dealt with liars before. Of course it could have been Steve the Cop who was the liar, but I didn't think so. My money was on Ferguson.

Now wasn't the time to press him, however. He was on his home ground. Besides, I didn't know a thing about him. He may have thought my "See you" was a casual good-bye, but it wasn't. I'd find out things, learn which buttons I could press, and then for sure I'd be seeing him again. He might not tell me the truth then, either, but at least I'd have some kind of handle. I was sure Dino could help me find one.

I went out through the downstairs, past the blasting sound of Amyl Nitrate, past the drinkers, past the few dancers. The night was chilly, and the humidity hung in the air like a wet sheet. I was almost to where I'd parked the Subaru before I noticed that it was gone.

One reason I drive a '79 Subaru is that it's cheap and it gets me where I want to go. But another reason is that while Houston and Dallas probably average something like one stolen car a minute, no one would ever want to steal an old Subaru with dead paint and a dented back bumper. The thieves go in for things like Camaros and Suburbans, never faded little Japanese jobs that look about ready for the scrap heap.

There was a black Ford parked where my car had been. I looked at it and then looked around the parking lot. Sure enough, there was the Subaru, pushed off to one side, about twenty yards away. I never bothered to lock the doors. There was nothing inside worth stealing.

I thought for a second about going back inside, rousting the owner of the Ford, and telling him what I thought of him. If he'd wanted a close parking spot, he could have waited for one. He didn't have to roll my car away.

But the confrontation wouldn't be worth the effort. It might make me feel better, but then again it might not. The owner might be bigger than me and decide that he'd like to hit me with his bicycle chain. I wasn't up to it.

I headed on over to the car. I was reaching for the door handle when three guys came around from the darkness on the other side.

I have no idea how the three of them managed to hide there. I wouldn't have thought the car was big enough to conceal them. They looked like the down linemen for the Chicago Bears.

One thing I have to give them credit for: they didn't mess around. No fancy words of warning, no shilly-shallying.

The one in the lead popped me in the stomach with a short right. He didn't have on a boxing glove, but his fist felt about the size of one.

I sort of folded up, and the other two each grabbed an arm, which was more than just a considerate gesture to make sure I didn't fall down.

The first guy hit me again, in the solar plexus this time.

I was sucking for air when he hit me the third time, in the stomach again. There was no way I could tighten up. I just took it. The two guys on either side of me held me upright.

That was their first mistake. Another mistake was in not doing me in right at the beginning. They should have cold-cocked me. I'm just crazy enough to fight back as long as I'm conscious.

So I kicked the guy in front of me in the balls.

He was surprised as hell. His eyes bugged out of his head and suddenly he was the one sucking wind. I guess he thought more of his punching than I did. Maybe he thought he *had* cold-cocked me.

He doubled over, clutching at himself and gagging. I jerked both arms, hard, trying to get free from the other two tough boys.

It didn't work. Kicking their buddy had been *my* mistake. I'd made them mad. Their hands were like iron bands on my arms and wrists.

They gave me a little swing forward; then suddenly the one on the right let go and chopped down at my knee with his fist. It probably wasn't exceeding the speed of sound when it hit.

He hit just the right spot. It was like someone had poked a hot iron rod into my knee, right under the kneecap. I gave a strangled, screaming shout. Anyone inside hearing it would think I was auditioning for Amyl Nitrate and the Whippets.

The guy on my left held me up until the one on my right could grab my arm again. The one on the left then grabbed the nape of my neck, forced my head down, and then they ran me—or dragged me—right into the side of my own car with all the force they had.

They had plenty.

This time they both let me go, and I sort of slid down the side of the car to the hard-packed dirt and gravel of the parking lot. They left me there and went to their buddy, who was only a step or two away.

I reached a hand up, trying to find something to hang onto and pull myself off the ground. One of them came over and clubbed me in the side of the neck. I went back down, and this time I didn't even think about trying to get up.

All three of them were standing over me. One of them was

still having a little trouble breathing, which was a small comfort to me. A very small comfort. One of the others took any pleasure I had in it away by kicking me three or four times in the ribs. He was wearing boots, and the pointed toes struck me sharply, like a blunt knife blade.

Then they patted me down. I thought they were looking for my billfold, but I was wrong. They stopped with the picture of Sharon Matthews. They looked at it, and then one of them began folding and tearing it into tiny pieces. I wouldn't have thought he could tear it so many times. It was pretty thick at the end. But then he was pretty strong. He dropped all the pieces and they sifted down on my chest. It was like watching them fall in a slow-motion movie.

During all of this, no one said a word. But no one had to. I was getting the message.

I thought they might start kicking me again, but just then a car turned into the lot, sweeping its headlights over them. They faded back into the darkness, and I could hear them moving away. I guess it hadn't been their Ford in my parking spot.

The car that had turned in came to a stop, and I heard a door slam. I still didn't feel much like getting up.

Before long, there was a man standing over me. He had what appeared to be a normal-looking haircut, but when he bent over to get a better look at me, a ponytail fell over his shoulder. I couldn't really tell in the bad light and in my feeble condition, but it looked as if it might have been dyed blue.

"Hey, man, you OK?" he said.

"M-ugg-unmph," I said.

"Sure, man. I'll help you get up." He reached down and put his hands under my armpits.

He pulled up, and I tried to stand. I thought I could manage all right as long as I didn't put any weight on the knee. I stuck out a hand and leaned on the car.

"How you feelin', man?"

I took a deep breath. It hurt, but I didn't think I had any broken ribs. Cracked, maybe. "Like six pounds of shit in a five pound bag," I said.

"Yeah. I know what you mean. Did they get your money?"

I told him they hadn't taken my money. "You got here just in time."

"You want me to call an ambulance? The cops, maybe?"

I opened the car door and sat in the seat, my legs sticking out into the parking lot. "No, thanks," I said. "I think I'll just go on home. You scared them off before they did any real damage." I twisted around, which hurt like hell, and took my billfold out of my back pocket. "See? Money all still here. And the cops'd never catch those three."

"Yeah, you got that right. You sure you're all right, though? You don't look so good."

"No blood, right? I must be OK if there's no blood."

He didn't look convinced, but he said, "Well, if that's the way you want it."

"That's the way I want it. Go on in and enjoy the band. They're really cooking tonight."

"They're cookin' every night," he said. "I guess I'll go, then." He started on across the lot. He looked back a couple of times, and I waved a jaunty hand at him. Then he was inside.

I just sat there for a while, maybe fifteen minutes. A couple of other cars came in, a couple left. No one paid me any attention. The three goons didn't come back.

Finally I got myself turned around and completely inside the car. I tested my right leg. I could work the accelerator all right, so I cranked up the engine and drove away from there, hauling what was left of me back to the Island.

8

RIGHT THEN I COULDN'T have beat the truth out of Pee-wee Herman or I might have gone back inside The Sidepocket and tried to beat it out of Ferguson. I wondered why Ferguson hadn't picked a nicer way of telling me to lay off instead of being so stupid and obvious. After all, I might have believed his lies. How was he to know I hadn't? Now I'd be certain to follow up on him.

I got back to the Island and drove to the house. Nameless was nowhere in sight. Just like a cat, thinking only of himself. Who was going to help me get up the stairs?

I managed to swivel around and get my legs out the car door. Then I put my left foot down and stood up. Now all I had to do was hop over to the door. I managed to do that, too.

I looked around in the darkness for something to use as a cane or a crutch. I had a cane that I'd used years before, but it was somewhere up on the second floor where it was doing me no good at all.

There was a piece of an old one-by-four lying on the ground by the steps. I leaned down, balanced myself carefully with my hand on a step, and picked up the board. It was a little too short, but it would have to do.

I tried a couple of steps in the yard with it before attempting the stairs. If I didn't put my right foot down too solidly, I could walk without screaming. I was a pretty tough guy, all right.

Getting up the steps wasn't easy, but I did it. Just as I got the door open, Nameless streaked by me and into the house. Typical. Now he'd expect to be fed. There were times when I wished I were a cat. It must be nice to live a life of total irresponsibility. All you had to do was find some sucker to feed you.

Nameless meowed as I came hobbling in through the door. Clearly I wasn't living up to my obligation to get food in the bowl the instant he wanted it.

"Sorry," I said. "This is as fast as it gets. You want food, go find a rat."

Nameless meowed again, clearly not impressed with my excuse. I ripped open a bag of Tender Vittles and poured it in his bowl. He stabbed his head in as soon as I began pouring and grabbed a mouthful, purring now.

I hobbled on up to the second floor. Very slowly. When I got to the bed, I sat down and tossed away the board. The knee was hurting like hell, and my ribs weren't much better. I lay back on the bed, and against all the odds I went to sleep almost immediately.

Nameless woke me up. He jumped on the bed, walked up on my chest, and howled. It was completely dark, and I had no idea what time it was. I looked at my watch, punching the button that illuminated the numbers. 4:04. "Nameless," I said, "you can always be replaced."

"Wr-o-r-r-r." He stepped off my chest and jumped down from the bed.

I sat up. It wasn't so bad. I fumbled around on the floor until I located the board, then stood up. That wasn't so bad, either, but it was bad enough. Nevertheless, a man's gotta do what a man's gotta do.

I located the light switch. Nameless preceded me out of the room and down the stairs, his tail high. "I hope you have a nice time," I said as I opened the door on the first floor.

Nameless didn't say anything. He just left.

I went back upstairs. I hoped Dino had plenty of money. A thousand dollars wasn't going to be nearly enough. I'd earned that much with the knee. It was time to increase my rates.

I made it back upstairs, and this time I got undressed before I fell into the bed and into sleep.

I didn't even consider the usual morning run the next day, but the knee wasn't permanently damaged. It was a little swollen and tender, but that was all. It would never be as good as new, but then it hadn't been as good as new in a long time. The swelling would go down in a day or two, and I'd be back on the seawall in a day or two more. My ribs and stomach were sore, too, and I had some interesting bruises beginning to take shape. Soon they'd all merge into one big, colorful, liverish splotch, roughly in the shape of Australia, and almost as large. Nothing was broken, though; nothing was even cracked. The guys who had worked me over were real professionals.

The knee was the main thing, but if I was careful, it would be all right, or as all right as it had been since my last appearance on a football field.

After we'd wowed 'em in high school, Dino, Ray, and I had gone our separate athletic ways. Dino wanted to get away from the humid summers and winters of the Gulf Coast to a place where there were no palm trees and where he could see snow in the winter. As a result, he'd wound up in Lubbock, playing middle linebacker for Texas Tech, where he became an all-conference player his senior year. Meanwhile, I went to the University of Texas at Austin.

Ray, on the other hand, didn't have much choice. A couple of the Southwest Conference schools were beginning to let the first blacks on their teams at about that time, but Ray wasn't quite good enough to be in that small, elite number. He went instead to Prairie View A&M, an all-black school that had neither the academic nor the athletic prestige of the big-time programs in the state, some of which might have taken Ray if they'd only known how good he was going to become.

They didn't, so he was stuck. But he got bigger, and at the same time he got faster. He led the nation in interceptions his senior year, and Houston drafted him. He was in a car accident right after the draft. Some buddy who also got picked and had celebrated a little too long and too hard was driving, not that it mattered to Ray.

His legs healed fine, but in the process he lost a step. Not even that much. Half a step. But it was enough. He could run me or Dino into the ground, but that didn't matter. In the pros that half step can make all the difference. Ray lost it.

I lost it a lot sooner. It was one of those great days for football in Austin, about sixty degrees, not a cloud to be seen, that unidentifiable smell of fall in the air. A stadium full of screaming fans.

I went into the Texas Tech game leading the nation in rushing as a sophomore. People were already talking about the Heisman, if not that year, then the next one for sure. Agents were already making discreet and not-so-discreet inquiries. There was not a doubt in anyone's mind that I would be a millionaire after two more seasons.

Unless, of course, something disastrous happened.

The first three quarters of the Tech game went just fine. I'd gained over a hundred yards already, though it hadn't been easy. A lot of it had come on one play, a sweep around the right end. I'd broken loose at my own forty and gone untouched into the end zone. The rest of it had been ground out two or three yards at a time, and as often as not the one on top of me when they unstacked the tacklers was Dino.

He was double tough that day.

In the fourth quarter we were leading, twenty-one to eighteen, and we had the ball on the fifty. The quarterback called the sweep around the right end again.

I took the handoff and cut back, running parallel to the line of scrimmage. I could see the sideline in front of me, and just then a hole opened up to my left. I planted my right foot to make the cut; that's when Dino hit me.

I don't know to this day where he came from. I know I sure as hell didn't see him. I've watched the film since, and I still can't figure it out.

At any rate, he came in low, sailing through the air, and he was coming fast. When his helmet hit my knee, it sounded like a baseball bat hitting a watermelon. I've heard at least one guy who was sitting in the top row of the stadium say he was sickened by the sound.

Mainly what I remember after that is rolling around on the grass—there was real grass in Memorial Stadium then—and thinking that I'd been shot or something. I remember seeing Dino standing above me, his helmet off. I think he was crying, but he's never mentioned it, and neither have I.

A couple of operations and lots of rehab later, I could walk just fine. But I never played football again.

I tried. It took nearly two years to get ready, but in my senior year I went out for practice. The coaches gave me every chance. But it was no use. I was slow. I couldn't cut. And worst of all, I knew that if anyone hit me on that knee again, especially if they hit me as hard as Dino had, I'd be hobbling for the rest of my life. If I was lucky. If I wasn't, I'd be a cripple.

I was bitter about it for a while. Who wouldn't be? I wasn't cut out to be one of those sunshiny guys who talks about how everything happened for the best in this best of all possible worlds.

At least they let me keep my scholarship. I took all the

right courses and graduated with my class, which was more than I could say for most of the guys I'd played with.

I started law school, then dropped out, but a lawyer I'd gotten to know asked me to do a few jobs for him. It turned out that I was pretty good at investigations, especially finding people, a job that paid pretty well in the runaway days of the early 1970s.

Dino and I had lost touch, until I finally came back to Galveston to look for Jan. He'd been there all along, joined by Ray after his brief fling with the pros (two weeks of training camp was as long as he lasted), and there they still were.

Jan was in the stands the day my knee was ruined. She was just a kid then, and she and I laughed about it in the hospital afterward, about how I'd have to stop being a dumb jock and learn a useful trade. I'd learned a trade, all right, but it hadn't been useful to her. I wondered if I'd ever see her again, or if I'd ever stop wondering what had happened to her. Now that I'd become involved in the search for Sharon Matthews, my mind was not entirely on my own problems for a change; the job was good for me. As long as I managed to stay in one piece.

Since I wasn't going to be doing any running, I stayed in bed until I got bored, about nine o'clock. Then I got up and hopped over to the chiffonier. The cane was leaning up against one side of it, the same cane I'd bought when I got out of the hospital in Austin.

I'd been young and romantic, so I bought a romantic cane, hand-carved in Mexico, with a peacock and his long, colorful tail taking up most of the space, the design cut into the black varnished wood. What I'd liked best was the fact that the brass tip and the brass handle could be screwed off, the center of the cane removed, and the whole thing assembled into a pool cue. I'd never used the cue, but I liked the idea of having it.

With the help of the cane, I walked over to the window

nearest my bed. There were windows on every wall, the house having been built to take advantage of the Gulf breezes in a time when air-conditioning wasn't even a dream in the mind of some crazed inventor.

The sill of the window looked like the sill of every other window in the room, but it wasn't. There was a little catch under the front lip. I pressed the catch, and the sill lifted up and folded back on hidden hinges.

In the hollow underneath was my pistol.

As a young, romantic investigator who had once bought a cane that made into a pool cue, I'd decided that I should have an appropriate weapon. I'd finally found one I liked, a Mauser Parabellum. You might call it a Luger, but when Mauser began to make the gun again they discovered that somehow they didn't own the rights to that name, which doesn't appear on the pistol at all. It looks just like the original, though, except that it has a slimmer, longer barrel. The one I have uses 7.65 mm cartridges, but I never intended to shoot water buffalo with it. A 7.65 will bring a man down if you shoot him in the right place.

Of course I never intended to shoot anyone.

I took the leather sheepskin-lined case out of its hiding place and lowered the sill, pressing down until I heard the catch click. I took the case over to the bed, sat down, and opened the zipper. The Mauser looked just as deadly as ever.

I got dressed then, jeans and sweatshirt, and took the pistol into the kitchen, where I laid it on a small wooden table. I had some gun oil in the cabinet, along with some rags and a swab. I got them out and went back to the table, leaned the cane against it, and sat in a chair.

The pistol was easy to disassemble. It took about a minute and a half. I cleaned it carefully, oiled it, then put it back together.

Parabellum. The word meant *for war.* Well, if I met those guys from the parking lot again, it was going to be war, all right.

I stuck the gun in the waistband of my jeans and went back into the bedroom. There was a box of cartridges in the hiding place, too. I got them out and loaded the clip with seven of them, thought about it for a minute, jacked one into the chamber, and put the eighth into the clip. I didn't like to store them in the clip. I had a theory that it weakened the spring.

After I'd done all that, naturally I felt like a fool. I'd never shot anyone, and I really didn't think I was going to start now. I'd been to the firing range often enough, though not in the last year or so, and I was really pretty good with the Mauser; but I hoped I wouldn't have to use it.

Nevertheless, I felt better just having it around.

As I was stumping around the brass bed, trying to get the covers in some kind of order, I realized that I'd slept better last night than I had in quite some time.

Maybe I should go out and get beaten up more often.

Or maybe it was just that getting my mind somewhat off Jan was improving my sleep.

After the bed was made I went and sat on the sagging couch and tried to think about what to do next. The logical thing seemed to be to find out a little more about Chuck Ferguson. So I called Dino.

Ray answered, then put Dino on. I could hear the *Donahue* show in the background. "Phil got any weird ones on today?" I said.

"Just a bunch of people that claim they've been kidnapped by funny-looking guys in UFOs. Nothing new in that." His voice sounded a little ragged. "But you didn't call to talk about what's on TV, did you?"

"I went to The Sidepocket last night," I said. "Talked to Ferguson. I'd like to know a little more about him."

"Why? He know something?"

It could have been my imagination, but I thought there was an edge of real curiosity in his questions. "Says he doesn't know a thing," I said. "But you never can tell. Can you find out anything about him?"

"Gimme an hour. I'll call you."

"No, I'll call you. I'm looking into some other stuff, too."

I didn't say what the other stuff was, and I didn't mention the little scuffle of the previous evening. It wasn't that I didn't trust Dino, exactly; it was just that nothing was making sense and I didn't think it would be to my advantage to tell him everything right then. Even if it did mean putting off asking for that raise.

"What about Sharon?" Dino said. The edge was still there, even more pronounced if anything.

"I'll let you know as soon as I find out anything concrete. Right now, I'm just poking sticks in holes, seeing if anything jumps out at me."

"Call me back anytime after an hour, then."

"Right," I said. We hung up.

I realized then that I'd forgotten about Nameless. I went downstairs to let him in. It was easier going down than I thought it would be. The cane was much better than the board. I opened the door, and Nameless fell in as if his head had been pressed against it.

"Sorry," I said.

He looked at me reproachfully while I got his food.

I stood and watched him eat. Then we went upstairs, where he proceeded to jump up on the couch and groom himself, licking himself all over, then biting himself between the toes. Watching him made my tongue feel nasty.

I put some old 45s on the Voice of Music and listened to Creedence, the Beatles, and Buddy Holly while I tried to read a few more pages in the Faulkner book. I didn't accomplish much. The problems of Quentin Compson and Rosa Coldfield seemed pretty much far removed from what I was working on.

I put the book down. By then Nameless was sound asleep,

stretched out full length against the back of the couch.

Having called Dino and put him onto Ferguson, I had several new options. I could try talking to Julie Gregg again. I could call Vicky Bryan and try to find out more about Terry Shelton. That was an attractive idea, but it involved prying into the murder case. I definitely liked the thought of Vicky, but I definitely disliked the idea of tangling with Barnes. I could call Evelyn Matthews, but she would see me only after she got off work, and it was much too early.

It had to be Julie Gregg, though I certainly hadn't ruled Vicky out. I would get back to her later. I grabbed up Nameless, who clearly didn't appreciate it, held him in one arm, and made my way down the stairs to the car. I put Nameless down and thought about the gun.

Texas gun laws are a little strange. I'm sure most New Yorkers think that armed Texans walk the streets of every city and town in the state, but that's just not true. Only the cops can carry a pistol. Legally. You can't even carry one in your car unless you lock it in the trunk, and you certainly can't carry one on your person. Legally.

Now what good a pistol would do me if it were locked in the trunk of my car, I couldn't imagine. So I wasn't going to put it there. At the same time, I wasn't going to carry it tucked into my jeans.

I compromised by wrapping it in an old towel that I carry around to wipe the dew off my windshield on days when the humidity is bad—nearly every day, in other words. If I was stopped and the car was searched, I was going to be in big trouble. It was a risk I'd just have to take. And I was pretty sure that if I went back to The Sidepocket, the pistol would be stuck in the waistband. I wasn't eager to meet Ferguson's little pals again unless I was armed.

I started the car and headed for the college.

9

I STOPPED FOR A Schlotsky's sandwich on the way. I was either going to have to buy some groceries or get all my vital nutrients from fast food. I thought for a second about buying some vitamin pills, but it was only a thought.

I got lucky again. Julie Gregg was in the same office, stapling some more papers. It was almost as if no time at all had passed in her world.

She looked up at me, then back down at the papers. I could tell that she wasn't pleased to see me.

"Hi," I said, leaning on my cane. I hoped it gave me a rakish look.

She stared at me with her wide blue eyes, but she didn't speak.

"Look," I said. "I'm not really any more thrilled about this than you are, but I have to talk to you again. Sharon is still missing."

"So?"

It wasn't much, but it was a start. "So a boy she knew, Terry Shelton, turned up dead yesterday. Maybe you heard about it. He was murdered."

The wide eyes got even wider. She hadn't heard. "I found

80

out that he and Sharon used to go to Houston, to a club called The Sidepocket, but that's all I found out. Sharon could be in real trouble, Julie. You may be able to help her."

"I really don't know very much," she said. The defiance was gone out of her. Death sometimes has a way of affecting the young like that, especially when it's someone young who's died, and especially when the death is sudden and unexpected. And violent.

"You know more than I do," I said. "Anything at all might help."

She thought about it. "OK. I don't know who told her about her mother, if that's what you want. She came in one day, really upset, and we talked about it. But she didn't say how she knew."

"When was that?"

"About two weeks ago, I guess."

"And just how upset did she seem?"

Julie shook her head. "That's what I don't understand. She was upset, like I said, but she wasn't crazy or anything. I mean it wasn't like she was thinking of suicide or something like that. She was mostly just mad that her mother hadn't told her before."

"But she didn't say how she found out?"

"No."

"Then we won't worry about it. What about this Terry Shelton?"

"I met him once. He didn't go to school. He worked down on The Strand somewhere, but he came up here on his lunch hour one day to visit Sharon."

"What was your impression of him?"

She tried not to look disapproving, and failed. "He wasn't very mature. He thought he could just manage to get by on his salary, which I bet wasn't very much, until someday his big opportunity came along. I don't know where he thought he was going to get a big opportunity in this place." She looked around the room, but that wasn't the place she meant. She meant the Island, or maybe the whole Gulf Coast.

"Did you find out anything about him? His family, where he lived?"

"I got the impression that he's not BOI," she said. "I think he's from Houston, but his parents have a place over on Bolivar. That's where he's staying." She caught herself. "Where he *was* staying."

Bolivar Peninsula isn't far from Galveston, just across the bay, but the only way to reach it is by ferry. Unless you want to go the long, long way around. The state runs the ferry service, and if you don't make the trip on a weekend, the wait usually isn't too long. The boats run every fifteen minutes. I could find out Shelton's address from his employer if I had to.

"One more thing," I said. "No one's seen Sharon since last Friday. Was she in school that day?"

"I think so," Julie said. "That's the day we had a test in government class, and we got them back today. The teacher called her name when he was passing them out, so she must have taken the test."

"Did she seem nervous that day, anxious about anything?"

"You mean besides the test? No, I don't think so. I don't remember anything different about her at all."

"Think about it," I said. "Think hard. Did she say anything? Did she mention Terry?"

She brightened, and I could have kicked myself. Leading the witness, that's what they call it in court. No matter what she said now, if it involved Terry Shelton, I'd wonder if she really recalled it or if I'd prodded her into a false memory.

"I do remember something," she said. "Right after the test we went to the soft drink machine for a Pepsi. She said something about having a date with Terry that night, but that it would be a lot different from their usual dates. I asked what she meant, but she said she couldn't tell me. She seemed a little excited, but not nervous or anything."

"And she didn't tell you anything more about it?"

"No. We just drank the Pepsis and that was it. She went off to another class."

I leaned against the door frame and thought about what Julie had said. It sounded as though she was telling the truth and not just creating a memory to please me. Everything seemed to be forcing me more and more toward the murder, as much as I wanted to avoid it.

"Thanks, Julie," I said. "You've been a help." I turned to go.

Her voice stopped me. "Do you think Sharon's . . . all right?"

"Sure," I said over my shoulder. "She'll probably be back in school in a few days."

"I hope so," she said.

I went on down the hall, thinking that our dialogue had almost reversed itself since our first talk. The trouble was, this time I was trying to string her along. After everything that had happened, I really didn't think she'd ever see Sharon Matthews again.

I located a pay phone and called Dino. Ray answered. When I identified myself, he said that Dino wanted to talk to me.

"Tru?" Dino said when he came on.

"That's me," I said.

"I got that information you wanted. It may mean something to you. It does to me, but I don't know what."

"So tell me."

"That Chuck Ferguson does own The Sidepocket. Ray and me, we never heard of him, that's why Ray said he couldn't be sure who really owned it. Anyway, here's the funny part. Until a few months ago, Ferguson was just the manager. The club was owned by Jimmie Hargis. You heard of him?"

I'd heard of him. He was a big name in low circles. He owned a few "straight" clubs, but mostly his name made the news when the cops closed down one or another of his peep shows or nude bars.

"I've never met the man," I said. "What about you?"

"I've met him. And this is straight from the horse's mouth. Ferguson bought him out."

"You mean Ferguson bought everything Hargis owned?"

"No, no. Just that one club. But it's still funny."

"Why?"

"Because Ferguson is just a small-timer. Just a guy who runs a place. Where does he get the money to buy a club from somebody like Hargis?"

"That's a good question," I said. "You got the answer?"

"Hargis didn't ask Ferguson any questions. I guess you know how that goes. He was just glad to get the money, times being what they are."

What Dino meant was that the city of Houston was cracking down on the topless clubs and peep shows and Hargis was having his own version of a money crunch.

"So it was a cash sale?"

"That's right. Except that Hargis had to loan Ferguson the money for a while. He didn't say what the juice was, but you can bet it was plenty. Anyway, Ferguson met the payments. Paid everything off right on time. So now he owns the place."

I didn't say anything for a second or two.

"You still there?" Dino said.

"I'm still here. Just thinking."

"I want to know what this has to do with Sharon. I mean it sounds funny, all right, but so what?"

"I don't know yet," I said.

"Well, when *are* you gonna know?" Dino's voice was sharp with impatience.

"I don't know when. But I'll be in touch." I hung up the phone before he could say any more.

I went out to the parking lot. The weather had turned so

warm and humid that you'd hardly guess it was February. I pushed up the sleeves of my sweatshirt and opened the car door.

I hadn't been lying to Dino. I really had no idea what was going on, but I knew *something* was, something that had to do with the disappearance of Sharon Matthews. Eventually a pattern would begin to take shape, or I hoped that was what would happen. Until it did, there was nothing I could do but talk. Find out a little here, a little there, until things began to make some kind of sense.

I was nearly certain now that Sharon's disappearance and Terry Shelton's murder were somehow tied together, but I didn't know how. She'd gone missing at about the same time the murder had occurred, and they had been seen together at The Sidepocket talking to a man who now denied even knowing them. A man who had suddenly come into a good bit of cash money. But Sharon had also discovered some disturbing information about her family history at about the same time. How did that fit in? Or did it?

My theory was that there was always a reason for a disappearance. I'd never been able to find one in Jan's case, and that one thing bothered me more than any other. If there was no reason, none at all, then she was dead. But who had killed her? And where was her body?

I tried to stop thinking about Jan. She didn't have anything to do with Sharon Matthews.

It was still early afternoon. It was time to try tapping two of my pipelines into the gossip of the Island, two people who might have some inkling of things out of the ordinary. Usually these two would know more about adults than about troubled teenagers, but I didn't have any better sources to try. To tell the truth, I was beginning to suspect some of the adults were more involved than they were letting on.

One person who might know something lived right on Broadway, in a house that had been part of the city for well over a hundred years. Sally West's family wasn't one of the Big Three families that had built the Island, but her roots went almost back to Galveston's beginnings. Her ancestors hadn't amassed quite the fortunes others had nor had they attained quite the fame, but the people who counted knew about them. Sally was the last of the line. Her husband had died young, and she had refused to marry again, thus leaving no descendants. Instead she lived in decaying splendor and kept up with everything that happened through a series of visitors, most of whom hoped to get some of her money in one way or another.

Dino had introduced me to her, and I was something of a novelty. All I wanted was information, not money or influence. Sally liked me, and I still dropped by every now and then to exchange information. That's what Sally called gossiping—exchanging information.

I stopped by a liquor store and bought a bottle of Mogen David wine. Despite her nearly patrician standing, Sally had modest tastes. With the wine in a plain brown paper sack I drove to her house, which was practically across the street from a fried-chicken franchise.

The house was red brick, built up high, with white latticework on the front porch. Wide concrete steps led from the ground level up to the porch. I mounted them and knocked at the screen. I'd left my cane in the car. I limped a bit, but not enough to matter.

An old black man opened the inner door. I had no idea how old he was; he might have been as old as Sally, who was eighty-nine. He might have been older. Or younger.

"Hello, John," I said.

"Hello, Mr. Truman," he said in the same way he might have addressed me had I shown up at the doorway a hundred years earlier. "Come in, sir."

I opened the screen and stepped in, handing him the wine. He took it, but neither of us mentioned it.

"Miz Sally's in the parlor," he said.

I walked a few steps down the high-ceilinged hallway, then turned through a wide double door to my right. There were worn throw rugs on the hardwood floor. The furniture was all wood, and there was a baby grand piano in the back of the room. A white lace piano shawl was draped over it. There were a reclining couch and a love seat and several wooden rockers with cane bottoms and backs. Sally West was sitting in one of them, rocking gently.

The light in the room was dimmed by white curtains at the window, but I could see her plainly. She was wearing a dark floor-length dress, and she had a shawl around her shoulders. Her hands gripped the arms of the rocker to help her propel it. If she stood, she would probably come up to about my belt, I thought, though I'd never seen her stand.

She looked up at me, her eyes bright in her wrinkled face. "Truman," she said. "How nice of you to drop by."

"Hello, Sally," I said. I felt a little shy, because I hadn't been to visit for quite a while.

"Don't stand there looking awkward," she said. "Come in and sit down." Her voice had a slight quaver in it, but you had to listen for it. Otherwise you might mistake it for the voice of a much younger woman.

I stepped into the parlor and sat in one of the rockers. Just about the time I got settled, John came into the room with the Mogen David on a silver tray. He had poured some of it into two crystal glasses. He offered the tray to Sally.

"Thank you, John," she said. "And thank you, Truman."

"You're welcome," I said. John brought the tray over to me, and I took the second glass.

"Leave the wine, please, John," Sally said. He put the tray on a small table near my chair.

I took a sip of the wine. It was a little too warm and a little too sweet for me, but what did I know? I drank Big Red.

"How have you been, Truman?" Sally asked after knocking back a hefty swallow of the wine. She liked it a lot more than I did.

"Fine," I said.

"I don't suppose you've come to tell me anything new about your sister?"

"No," I said. "This is about something else."

"I see." She took another swallow. "You're working again?"

"Yes," I said. "I'm working again. Not for myself this time."

"Good. I've often wondered if you would ever stop your brooding and get back on your feet."

"I was ready," I said. "I just needed a push."

"And who gave it to you?"

I told her.

"Ah, Dino. I knew his uncles well, of course. The Island was a different place in those days."

Her eyes drifted around the room. She had seen quite a few changes in her long life. On the wall, a little higher than the level of the piano, there was a black mark about six inches wide and a foot long. It indicated the level to which the water had risen in the storm of 1900. She hadn't seen that, but she hadn't missed it by much.

Her eyes came back to rest on my face. "And what are you doing for Dino? I do hope it's interesting."

"It is. But it's confidential."

She drank the last of the wine in her glass. I still hadn't taken a second swallow. "Confidential?" she said.

"I can tell you, but you can't tell anyone else."

"Oh, then, that's all right. As long as *I* know. Could you do me the favor . . . ?" She extended her glass, and I got up and refilled it.

I sat back down and told her the story, leaving out a little, but not much. I told her more than I'd told Dino about the fight at The Sidepocket.

"Goodness," she said. "Maybe you were better off when

you were vegetating there in that old house, doing a bit of painting to make ends meet."

"I'd forgotten what a sarcastic old lady you are," I said.

She laughed. "At my age, it's about all the aggression I have. Now, what do you think I know about any of this?"

"Not much. Maybe nothing. But there's one thing that's been bothering me. Why is Dino so interested in this Sharon Matthews? I know that her mother was one of his uncles' girls, and I can understand the concept of family loyalty, up to a point. But he's really worried about this. If you could talk to him, you'd know what I mean. You can hear it in his voice."

"Dino doesn't get out much," she said. "I was afraid for a time that you might become like that."

"I've wondered about him," I said. "Does he ever leave that house?"

"Hardly ever. He's become like me, though he is not so much a prisoner of his body as his mind."

"Come again?"

"You've been away from the Island for quite a while, haven't you? Too long, really, for you to have noticed, I suppose."

I couldn't quite make out her meaning. "I guess I'm not following you exactly," I said.

"What do you remember most about when you were young? Most about the Island, I mean, not about yourself."

I thought about that for a minute. "I don't really know," I said finally. "Times seemed better then, but maybe I was just younger."

"No," she said. "Times were better then. And they were even better before that. When my family came here, Galveston was the largest city in Texas, the most civilized. The first electric lights in the state? The first telephones? We had them here. Why, Houston was nothing more than a mudhole—not that it's improved much. But time has passed the Island by. And people like me, people who can remember the old days, we hide in our houses so that we won't have to go outside and see what the Island has become." She paused and drained her wineglass.

"But the preservation that's begun—"

"Most of it by people who weren't even BOI," she said. "Or who at least have not lived here for quite some time, who made their money elsewhere."

She extended her glass. I refilled it. "But Dino?" I said.

"Dino is like me, in a way, I think. He knows better than anyone how much his uncles meant to this town, how much money they brought in with their women and their night-clubs and their casinos. For him, those are the Island's glory days, just as for me those days are further in the past. He can no more bring them back than I can, and he is just as afraid to try. How can anyone live up to a legend? He would only doom himself to fail. And so he lives his life in his house, as I do."

"He wasn't always like that," I said.

"No," she said. "Once he was young."

"He still is," I said, thinking of myself.

"In a way, perhaps. Much younger than I, at any rate. And both of you may live to see the return of some of this place's former glory. I'm afraid that I never shall, however. But never mind. You were asking for other information, and I've rambled on like the old woman I am. Where were we?"

I wasn't sure that she had been rambling at all. In fact, I was almost certain that she believed that in some way her words were a pertinent part of our discussion. And maybe they were.

"We were talking about a girl named Sharon Matthews," I said. "And about why Dino is so worried about her."

"Yes, of course. How could I forget? Well. I suppose you know that an old woman like me, who lives alone and keeps to herself, does have some visitors who might tell her a thing or two."

She smiled. She knew that I was counting on her hunger for gossip. Let the town decay as fast as it might, she would try to learn every detail of its decadence.

I smiled too. "Yes," I said. "I know."

"Of course. Now think about it. How old is this girl?"

I told her again.

"Which means that she was born when? In relation to Dino's career?"

"Just about the time he graduated from college. But—" Then I saw where she was going. I set my still nearly full wineglass down on the tray. I was afraid my hand would shake and spill some of the wine. "It's not possible," I said.

"Of course it is. Anything's possible."

"But Evelyn Matthews told me she was on the circuit when she got pregnant." Something else came to me then. I was getting soft in the head. "But that's not what Dino said. He said she'd stayed here on the Island after the houses closed down. Damn. They didn't even have their stories straight."

"I don't know for sure," Sally said. "It was only a vague rumor, at best, even when it was fresh. I haven't heard a word about it in years and years."

"So you *can* keep a secret."

"That's why so many people like to talk to me," she said, and smiled.

$\triangledown$

1 0

WHEN I STEPPED BACK out into the twentieth century, the day had turned dark and sour. Heavy, dark clouds had pushed in from somewhere, and a thin, drizzly rain was falling.

I had to talk to Dino, which meant that I wouldn't be calling Vicky Bryan. I also wouldn't be talking to my other source, who wouldn't be out in this kind of weather. That part was all right, but I really wanted to talk to Vicky, and not necessarily about the case. Maybe tomorrow.

I wasn't angry with Dino, not exactly. I'd been lied to enough times in the past to more or less expect it. It always complicates things, though. It alters the feeling about the case, and it opens up new directions when things should be settling into an understandable pattern. The truth is always easier, if not more agreeable.

Ray met me at the door. "He's been trying to call you."

"Yeah. Well, I have a few things to say to him, too." I walked into the living room, hardly limping at all. I would never let Dino see me using the cane.

The video equipment was silent, perhaps because there was another person with Dino in the room. Evelyn Matthews. I was a little surprised to see her, and the surprise must have showed on my face.

"I gotta tell you a couple of things," Dino said. "You better sit down."

"I think I know what you want to say," I told him. "Why didn't you tell me sooner?"

I looked at Evelyn, who was smoking, sitting near the coffee table so that she could tap her ashes into a cheap metal ashtray that Ray must have rounded up from somewhere.

Dino watched me watching Evelyn. "So you know. I should've known you'd find out. I knew you were good when I hired you."

I sat down. "You should have told me."

"I know," he said. "I was dumb. I just thought you didn't need to know."

"That's why there was all the urgency," I said. "I knew you weren't the most humanitarian guy on the Island."

"It's more urgent now than it was then," he said.

"Why?"

"You tell him," Dino said.

Evelyn stubbed out her cigarette. "At first we thought it was just one of those things, that Sharon left because of what she found out about me. But it wasn't that. If it were, Sharon would have gotten in touch by now. She hasn't. Someone else has."

Damn, I thought.

"Let me tell it," Dino said. "There was a phone call today. Came here, to the house—"

"Wait a minute," I said. "We're going to have to begin at the beginning. Sharon's your daughter, right?"

"That's right," Dino said. "I—"

"And how many people know that?" I asked.

Evelyn lit another cigarette. She was right. She did smoke too much. "Hardly anyone," she said, exhaling a cloud of smoke.

"How did you find out, anyway?" Dino said.

"Never mind that. Obviously it's not a complete secret. There was talk at one time, at least according to my source. How much contact have you had with Evelyn and Sharon over the years?"

"None," Dino said. "Well, hardly any. It wasn't like Evelyn and I were in love or something."

"So where did Sharon come from?"

"Evelyn and I ran into each other one evening after I got out of college. I was remembering the old days. You know. Evelyn wasn't in the game anymore, but we'd both had a couple of drinks—"

"—and that's all there was to that," Evelyn said. "I got careless, but I've never regretted it. And I've never accepted a penny from Dino. Not a penny." She jabbed the air with her cigarette to emphasize her point.

"Evelyn's never even been to this house before," Dino said. "I called her now and then, and I kept up with the kid. But that's all. And now someone wants me to pay for it. Goddamn it, how did anyone find out?"

"This is a small island, and a small town," I said. "People talk. I imagine you were a hot topic, nineteen or twenty years ago when you came back here. Anyway, it doesn't matter. The question is, does the girl mean anything to you? Would you pay to get her back?"

Dino didn't look at Evelyn. "Of course I'd pay. I've got money."

"That's why someone called you, then. They wait a few days to get you on edge, then they call. What was the message?"

"Ray!" Dino said.

Ray appeared from some other room.

"You answered the phone," Dino said. "Tell him."

"Whoever it was wouldn't talk to me," Ray said. "It was a funny, deep voice, like someone was trying to disguise the way he talked. He said 'Let me talk to Dino.' I said, 'Who is this?' The guy said, 'Let me talk to Dino, or you'll both be sorry.' So I let him."

Dino took over. "He told me that he had a girl named Sharon Matthews. That nothing had happened to her yet, but that something would if I wasn't real careful. He said that if I called the cops, he'd kill her. Then he said he'd call again."

The warning had not been necessary. Coming from the background he had, Dino would never call the cops. But I felt I had to try to persuade him to call them.

"You know that the police, especially the FBI, are equipped for dealing with this kind of thing. You know they can handle it without creating any publicity. I think you ought to consider calling them."

Dino just looked at me.

"I've never worked on a kidnapping before," I said. "I could make some wrong moves. I could get her hurt."

"You don't have to worry about any wrong moves," Dino said. "I'm going to pay the money. They don't want you in it, either."

I felt a definite twinge in my knee. "They mentioned me?"

"They said something about keeping the snooper out of it, too." Dino was apologetic. "I won't ask you for any of the advance money back."

"Look, Dino, can't you see what's going on here? I think—"

"I'm sorry about this, Tru," he said. "But this is the way it's gotta be. I know I've been a pretty lousy guy, especially about Sharon, but I can't take a chance on killing her. I got to do what they say." Dino looked at Evelyn. "We've talked it over, and we think it's the best way."

Evelyn nodded her agreement.

I was frustrated, but I could see they'd made up their minds. I tried once more anyway. "Dino, there's more going on here than you think. There's been a murder, and it's tied in some way. You've got to let me do something."

"Just a second ago you said you never worked on a

kidnapping. Now you're an expert? Thanks, Tru, but no thanks. I'll do this their way. It's the way it's got to be."

I stood up. "OK, if that's what you want to do. I hope it all works out." I started out of the room.

"You're limping," Dino said. "The knee all right?"

"Sure," I said. "It's just the rain. Change in the weather." I didn't wait to see if he believed me. I went on out.

Ray was waiting by the door. "You out of it?"

"I'm out," I said.

"See you around."

"Sure," I said.

I sat in the Subaru for a few minutes and tried to think about what I was going to do next. The rain had stopped, and the sky had cleared a bit, but the late afternoon had turned to night. I could see stars between the ragged edges of the clouds, and a thin sliver of moon.

I told myself that in Dino's place I'd do the same thing he was doing, but it seemed obvious to me that the kidnapping was being orchestrated by someone I'd recently met, namely Chuck Ferguson. Where had he gotten the money he'd used to pay off Hargis? Did he need more? Why had he lied about knowing Sharon and Terry? How had the voice on the phone known about me? Dino didn't want to talk about things like that. After nearly twenty years of neglect, he'd finally decided to play daddy and save his daughter the only way he knew how, with his money.

Knowing all that, I thought I should probably go to Gerald Barnes and lay it out for him. Somehow Ferguson had to be tied in to the murder of Terry Shelton, who, after all, had been out walking around free as the air while his girlfriend was being held somewhere by kidnappers. Had Shelton been in on it, too? Barnes could figure it all out, and I could go back to painting houses. That was what I was good for, after all.

But if I went to Barnes and he fouled up Dino's payoff,

then I'd really be in trouble with Dino, and maybe even be risking Sharon's life. So telling Barnes was out. I'd let Dino handle it his way. What the hell. I still had most of the thousand dollars, and I hadn't done much more to earn it than take a pretty good beating. And the knee wasn't bothering me that much now. So I could go home with a clear conscience, which is what I finally did.

Still, it pissed me off.

I fed Nameless, who sped right back out again in pursuit of whatever it was he pursued all night, and got up the stairs without the aid of the cane. Then I looked up Vicky Bryan's number in the phone book and called her. One thing about being off the case—my time was now my own.

She answered on the third ring, but when I told her who it was she didn't sound impressed. In fact, a weak "Oh" was all she said.

"Hey," I said. "I know I'm no Tom Cruise, but I'm taller than he is. And I can wiggle my ears."

She warmed up just a little. "I bet you can't."

"Sure I can. Let me take you to dinner, and I'll prove it."

She was still hesitant. "I didn't go in to work today. I was a little shook up over . . . you know."

"I know. I was too." I wasn't going to tell her anything about my involvement with Terry Shelton. After all, I was out of it. If the police had told her I was a guy looking for his sister, let her believe it. If they hadn't, I'd tell her something else. "There's no better way to get over a shock than to eat a good meal. I bet you haven't eaten all day."

She said I was right. Sort of. "Hardly anything, though. Just an apple and a piece of bread. And a glass of milk."

"Then you need something substantial. Don't dress up. I'll be there in fifteen minutes."

"Well, all right. But give me an hour."

In exactly fifty-nine minutes I was knocking on her door.

She lived in a small apartment over a garage on 0-1/2 Street. More stairs, but I hardly noticed them. I realized that I hadn't been out with a woman since I started looking for Jan. A year is a long time.

She opened the door and stepped out. I like someone who's on time. She was dressed in jeans and a polo shirt. There was no little alligator or polo player on the shirt, so it probably wasn't expensive, but you could never tell about that.

"Are you sure you're taller than Tom Cruise?" she said.

"Of course I am. Trust me."

"OK. So wiggle your ears."

"I'll wait until we get where the light is better. You'll be more impressed."

She said she could wait, so we went down the stairs. She didn't wince when she saw the Subaru, which was another point in her favor.

"You don't exactly drive Tom Cruise's car, either," she said as I helped her in.

I went around to the other side and slipped under the wheel. "Or have his income. Let's face it, this is reality."

"You do have enough money for dinner, I hope."

"If you don't get carried away," I said.

She laughed. "I'll try to watch it."

I started the car and we drove up to the seawall, to Gaido's. "I have a craving for shrimp creole," I said.

She opened her door. "Sounds good to me."

Gaido's is one of the best seafood restaurants in Galveston, which means it's one of the best anywhere. It also has a giant crab crouching over the doorway. The waiters wear tuxes, but that doesn't mean the diners have to. We talked, and I found out that Vicky had an interesting story. She'd come to Galveston on spring break from Southwest Texas State University six years before and decided to stay, for reasons practically opposite those Dino had given for going to Texas Tech.

"I'm from West Texas," she said, "where it never rains and where people complain if the humidity gets over thirty percent. If it gets to ninety percent, they think they've had a flood." Everything about the Island, from the climate to the people, was so different from everything she'd known before that she wanted to be a part of it. "So I just went looking for a job instead of going back to school. My parents couldn't figure it out. I didn't try to. I just knew that I wanted to live here for a while. So far I haven't been sorry, but I am thinking of going back to school next fall."

"To Southwest Texas?"

"No, to A&M." She smiled. "I think I'll study marine biology."

I liked to see her smile. She had white, even teeth and a way of turning her head that gave her a slightly quizzical look. "I'm glad A&M has a branch here in Galveston," I said.

"Me too."

The shrimp creole came about that time, and we ate. I had no trouble cleaning out the white oblong bowl, and neither did Vicky. When we got back in the car, she asked about me. I told her about Jan. Then I told her a little about Terry Shelton.

I'd promised myself I wouldn't, but the more I thought about things, the worse I felt. Dino was being taken, and I thought I could have helped. Besides, I thought I could have found Sharon Matthews, which might in some way have made up for not finding Jan. So I told Vicky a little of it.

"You're a detective, then?"

"Only sometimes." I was driving along Seawall Boulevard, past the new Holiday Inn and the huge San Luis Hotel. Soon we'd be beyond the seawall, on the western part of the Island.

"And you think that Terry's death might have something to do with this girl you're looking for?"

"That's right, but I'm not sure what. Did you ever see a girl with him? Did one ever visit him at the store?"

"I don't remember," she said. "I don't think so. We didn't

talk much, and mostly he just talked about his parents' beach house on Bolivar. I think he might have wanted me to visit him there, but he was too shy to come right out and say it."

I wouldn't have blamed him for wanting Vicky to come for a visit, but I was more interested in the beach house itself. "Why did he live there? Why not with his parents?"

She shook her head. "I'm not sure. I don't think they liked his friends, the heavy metal bit. Like I said, he was a little old for that sort of thing. So I guess he just moved out to be on his own. After all, he was old enough."

Sure, I thought. On his own. With his parents still providing him with a rent-free house and probably spending money besides. "Do you know where the house is?" I asked.

"Not exactly. I got the impression it wasn't far from Bolivar, though."

Bolivar, located quite near the ferry landing, was the little town with the same name as the peninsula. Well, it still wasn't any of my business, but I would have liked to get a look in that house.

I turned right at Eight Mile Road and took Vicky home. We shared a chaste kiss at the top of her stairs, but I had a feeling that better things were in store, even if I was a good twelve or more years older than she was. I told her I'd call her soon. She didn't object.

When I got home, Nameless was nowhere around. I went up and read for a few minutes, then tried to sleep. It wasn't much good. I'd drift off for a second or two, and dreams of Sharon and Jan would wake me up. There were some dreams in which Jan was Sharon and some in which Sharon was Jan. Every time I woke up, I was sweating.

So I was still pretty much awake when the telephone rang somewhere in the neighborhood of three o'clock. I got it on the first ring.

The caller was Evelyn Matthews. "Can you come to my house?" she said. "Dino's been shot."

$\triangledown$

1 1

I DIDN'T ASK ANY questions. I just said I'd be there. As I put on my jeans, I wondered what had happened. Dino had ventured out of his house, for the first time in who knows how long, and look at the results. Now he might never go outside again. I wondered how badly he was hurt.

I also thought about how much I was on the way to becoming like Dino and Sally West. Like them, I'd pulled back into my shell, going out now and then to paint a house or for my morning run, but more and more staying at home when I could, letting all the food disappear before I'd go to the store for more. If I kept on long enough, I'd probably even give up the running. Sally and Dino had someone to do the going for them; I didn't. That was probably the only reason I hadn't already become a recluse. If it hadn't been for Dino's getting me to look for Sharon, when would I have left the house again other than to run? It didn't bear too much thinking about. He'd gotten me out, and he'd gotten me interested. And now he'd been shot.

I went downstairs. When I opened the door, Nameless bolted in, nearly tripping me and causing a stab of pain in the knee. I didn't hold it against him. I took a few seconds to rip open a packet of food, watch him eat, and toss him back out.

When I stepped outside, I was struck by the peculiar odor of a coastal town, a mixture of dying hermit crabs, saltwater, and what I figured was probably diesel fuel. As often happens, the temperature hadn't dropped much with the darkness, and the humid air felt heavy and almost warm.

I had taken the pistol out of the car before going out with Vicky, but I had it with me now. When I got in, I shoved it under the seat. I didn't think I'd need it, but it was nice to know it was there. Since the pistol was wrapped in the towel, I used the car's wipers to clear the windshield. I'd have to guess what was behind me, but at that time of night there wasn't likely to be anything on the streets except me, not in February, not in the middle of the week.

It took me only a few minutes to drive to Evelyn Matthews's house. The streets were quiet and deserted; no lights showed in any of the homes nearby. Cars that wouldn't fit in the one-car garages were parked at the curb by neatly trimmed lawns that turned briefly green in my headlights, then turned black again. It had been a mild winter, as it nearly always was, and some of the people on this street had already had to mow their yards. The home owners were all quietly asleep now, never dreaming about what was happening in the house where the light was on.

I stopped in front and got out, leaving the pistol in the car. Evelyn came to the door before I could knock.

"Come in," she said. She shut the door behind me when I entered.

"How is he?"

"He'll be fine, I think. The doctor—"

"Doctor? At this time of night? For a gunshot wound?"

"Dino knew who to call. He's retired now. I think he used to do some work for the uncles."

"Of course," I said. "I should have known."

"Yes. Anyway, the doctor says that Dino was lucky. One bullet went right on through, at the shoulder. It didn't hit anything major. Another one took off a little bit of his forearm. I think both of them hurt him a lot, but he wouldn't let the doctor give him a sedative. He wants to talk to you." She gestured with her right hand. "He's in the bedroom."

I went down a very short hall and into an equally small bedroom. There was a lamp with what must have been a forty-watt bulb on an end table. That was all the light in the room, and it wasn't much. The lamp had a heavy shade. Still, it was light enough for me to see that Dino wasn't feeling any too well. He half-sat, half-lay on the bed against a stack of three pillows. He still had on his pants, but his shirt and his shoes were off. There was a wide white bandage wrapped across his chest and over his left shoulder, not stained too badly. Another was wrapped around his left arm.

"Hello, Dino," I said. "Wanna race?"

His face was twisted slightly with the pain, but his voice was clear. "Fuck you, Smith. I could take you any time."

"Sure," I said. "You want to tell me about it?"

"That's why you're here. Sit down."

The bedroom was so small there was no room for a chair in it. Aside from the double bed and the end table, there was only a tiny chest of drawers. I looked around, and just about that time Evelyn arrived with a folding bridge chair with a metal seat.

"Thanks," I said, taking it from her. I opened it and sat.

"It was a setup," Dino said.

"They take the money and kill you besides, huh? What about Sharon?"

"We'll get to her, but let's talk about the first part." His voice cracked slightly. He waited a second or two. "They didn't take the money."

"Why not?"

"I don't even think they wanted it. I'm going to try to tell you the whole thing. I got the money together. I have a little cash on hand. I put it all in a little suitcase."

I didn't interrupt to ask just how much cash, or how much he kept on hand.

"The guy on the phone told me to take the money out to Scholes Field, out past the runways, down by the bayou. There's a dirt road that runs back there and sort of peters out. You know where I mean?"

Scholes Field is known now as the Municipal Airport for some reason. It's not because any planes to speak of ever land there. It was built to serve Fort Crockett, and I've heard that the runways can handle a 747, but all they handle now is the grass that grows up through the cracks. No major airline serves Galveston.

"I'd guess it would be pretty deserted back there in the small hours," I said.

"Yeah. Well, you'd be right. You can see the lights of the cars on the causeway across the bayou, but that's about it."

Evelyn squeezed by my chair and wiped Dino's face with a damp cloth. I hadn't even noticed that he'd been sweating, but obviously the talking was an effort for him.

"I was told to come alone," he said. "But I said I'd have to have a driver. I haven't driven for a long time. They told me I could bring Evelyn."

"What about Ray?" I said.

"They told me to send Ray away, that there'd be someone watching the house. So I did."

Evelyn finished with the cloth, squeezed back by me, and left the room. I noticed that she wasn't smoking now.

"She drove," Dino said. "We got back there, in among some saw grass, and parked. A car came up behind us and blinked its lights, which was the signal. I got out to give them the money." He twisted a little on the bed. "That's when they started shooting."

"They didn't even ask for the money?" It was hard to believe.

"That's right. I don't know how many shots there were. First one hit me in the arm." He raised the bandaged arm slightly. "Next one got me here." He gestured to his shoulder. "Or maybe not. There may have been one or two misses. One of 'em hit the car, I know that. Whoever was shooting couldn't see too good with just the headlights, maybe. Anyway, I managed to get the suitcase up in front of my belly, which was a good thing, since the next one went right into it. Knocked me flat."

"This sounds like one of those stories that end with me asking 'How did you get away from there' and you saying 'I didn't.' "

He almost smiled. "I did, though. That Evelyn. She must've been out of the car before I knew what was going on. Dragged me back and shoved me in."

I looked at him, the former linebacker, about two-twenty-five, and thought about Evelyn. This time, he did smile.

"She's little, but she's stout. Got that car moving, tore out of there ninety to nothing, bounced up on the runway like she was at Daytona and laid rubber for a quarter of a mile. We were back here before you could say Jack Robinson. She had the blood stopped with towels and the doctor called before I could hardly give her his name. She's something else."

"So," I said. "What about Sharon?"

"That's the big one, all right. That's what I want you to find out. Need any more money? I got a whole suitcase full. 'Course some of it's got a bullet hole in the middle."

I thought about it. Earlier that night, or the previous night to be exact, I'd been morally outraged and considerably upset that Dino wanted me out of his way. Now that I had the chance to get mixed up in things again, I wasn't sure I wanted to. Things were getting too strange and dangerous.

Getting my knee clobbered was one thing. Getting shot was another.

But I was curious, too. "What the hell," I said.

"Good." His body seemed to relax a trifle.

"Does Ray know?" I asked.

"No. What Ray don't know, Ray can't tell. I'm not taking any more chances."

"What about Evelyn? Does she . . . ?" I didn't know exactly how to finish my question.

"She's gonna let me stay here." He had the grace to look a bit sheepish. Or maybe it was the pain. "I . . . well, hell, I've been rotten to her and to the kid, but they say it's never too late, don't they? Maybe even old Dino can get domestic."

It would be hard for him to get any more domestic than he was already, I thought. He was just considering trading Ray for Evelyn. I wondered what she thought of the idea, but I didn't ask.

"See if you can find the kid," he said. "I'd like the chance to get to know her a little. And find out what the hell is going on."

"I'll try," I said.

I talked to Evelyn in the living room before I left. She was going to give Dino the sedative and let him sleep.

"Did they try to follow you from the airport?"

"I don't know. I wasn't looking. But I don't think so."

They could find out where she lived easily enough, if they didn't know already. "Would you like for me to stay?"

"That's all right. I've got a shotgun, and I know how to use it. And I'm a light sleeper. If anyone tries to bother us, he'd better be quieter than a cat."

I asked to see the shotgun. It was an old double-barrel twelve gauge with a scarred wooden stock and flecks of rust along both the blued barrels.

"It's been in the back of the closet," she said when she

saw me looking dubiously at the rust spots. "But I cleaned it up, and the shells aren't but a year old."

I broke the gun and looked at the shiny brass of the partially ejected casings. I could smell the gun oil. "I don't think it'll blow up in your face," I said, snapping the gun back together. It was a good weapon for her, since it would almost certainly hit whoever she pointed it at; and if it didn't hurt him, it would scare the hell out of him. And since it was a twelve gauge, even one pellet was going to cause a good bit of damage if it hit anyone. I handed the gun back to her.

"I'll come back by tomorrow," I said. "Are you sure you want Dino here?"

She carried the gun over to the couch and laid it down. "I think so. It seems funny, but I really think he's as worried about Sharon as I am. I never pressed him about her; I never even took any of his money. I think he was hurt by that. Maybe he wanted to be involved with her and I cut him off because I thought he looked at me as a cheap whore." She shook her head. "Maybe we were both just stubborn. Anyway, I do want to help him, to take care of him."

"You've already saved his life," I said.

"Maybe. Do you have any idea what's going on?"

"Not a clue," I said.

I pushed it all around in my head when I got to my car. It was about four o'clock and still dark, and I sat there in the faint bluish glow of a streetlight, trying to make some sense out of everything that had happened. First it had looked like a simple runaway. Then it had turned into something that probably involved a murder. Then came the kidnapping angle. And now someone was trying to kill Dino without even collecting the ransom.

That last bit was what bothered me more than anything. No one had even asked Dino for the money. He was holding the suitcase where it could be clearly seen, but no one even appeared to have been interested. Someone had just started shooting.

It was time to go back to Houston for a little conversation with Chuck Ferguson. He was the only handle I had on the case. I was convinced he'd lied to me, if the cop that I thought was a cop was really a cop. And if the cop hadn't lied. I didn't think he had. There was something about Ferguson's whole manner that indicated to me he was hiding something. I wanted to find out what it was.

I started the car. The light was still on in Evelyn Matthews's house. I could picture her sitting on the couch, holding the shotgun in her lap. It was almost as big as she was, but I wouldn't want to be the one to try walking through that front door without permission.

I turned the car around on the narrow street, and as I passed under the streetlight I checked my digital watch. It was 4:09. I decided to pay Ferguson a visit before breakfast. One of the first things I wanted to talk to him about was where he had gotten the money to pay for The Sidepocket.

I zipped down Broadway, across the bridge, and onto the Gulf Freeway very quickly. There was a smattering of traffic, even at that ungodly hour, but not as much as there would be in thirty minutes or so when the morning rush would begin in earnest. Traffic would slow almost to a standstill around Almeda-Genoa Road. I was glad I would miss it.

I made good time all the way to the club, pushing the little Subaru for all it was worth. The nearby peep shows and motels still had their lights blinking on and off, advertising their wares, but there were few other cars on the street.

There were no cars at all in The Sidepocket's lot. The portable sign was still lighted, but there were no lights anywhere else. I was hoping that Ferguson lived in the room above the club. I wanted to catch him off guard, and a sleeping man is generally about as off guard as a man can get.

I stopped the car in front of the club and turned off my

lights. Before I got out I reached down under the seat and pulled out the towel-wrapped pistol. I unwrapped the Mauser and hefted it, tossing the towel onto the backseat. The gun's weight was reassuring, and I decided to take it with me just in case I met the three refugees from the Pro Bowl again. I stepped out of the car and stuck the pistol into my waistband. The sweatshirt covered it nicely.

I walked around to the back of the club. I was hoping there was a back entrance, not wanting to have to force my way into the front. The fewer chances I took, the better. Someone was sure to drive by, even this early.

It was darker in the back, without the benefit of all the lights from the various enterprises along the street. I didn't have any trouble finding the door, however.

Neither had someone else. The door was slightly ajar.

That bothered me. A lot. It was possible that Ferguson wasn't there, that he had gone elsewhere and that since he lived in such a posh, crime-free neighborhood he hadn't bothered to lock the door behind him. Maybe he was so sure he wouldn't be robbed that he hadn't even bothered to *shut* the door.

Somehow, I didn't think that was what had happened.

What I thought was that someone had been here before me. Maybe someone was still here.

I felt for the butt of the pistol through the thick cotton of the sweatshirt, but I didn't pull it from my belt. I was a good range shooter, but I hadn't had much practice using the pistol against someone who was shooting back. I didn't want to have to learn, either, unless it was absolutely necessary.

I stepped to one side and pushed the door gently with my right hand. It opened slowly and quietly. There was no other sound, except for the shushing of a car passing on Telephone Road. After a second or two I stepped inside.

There was a small open space not large enough to be called a foyer. That's where I was standing. It was very quiet, a far cry from the thundering of Amyl Nitrate's bass. In front of me was a staircase leading up to the second floor. The door I had pushed open did not lead into the main area of the club.

There was barely enough light for me to see the staircase. I looked up, but I couldn't make out anything at the top except deeper blackness. There was probably a closed door up there. I started up to see.

The steps were plain bare wood, but they didn't creak as I went up. Some carpenter had done a good job of nailing down the boards. I tested each step, putting my weight down on it completely before actually stepping up, but there was no problem.

It was very dark at the top. I felt for the door handle, and when I felt it under my fingers I turned it slowly. Again there was no sound.

I opened the door ever so slightly. There was no light in the upstairs area, but then I hadn't expected there to be. I hadn't seen any from the parking lot when I drove in.

There were lots of things I could do at this point. I could close the door and go on my merry way. Or I could open it all the way and walk right in. I could drag out my Mauser and go in like the cops always do in TV shows, crouched down with the pistol extended in front of me in a two-hand grip.

I decided to go in but to leave the pistol where it was. My thinking was that anyone who had been there must be gone by now. Otherwise there would have been a light. If Ferguson was there, he was probably asleep. I hoped.

I opened the door slowly and ran my hand down the wall, searching blindly for a light switch. My fingers ran across it, and I flipped it up. The hall was suddenly bright with light. All the doors were closed. I could see the one Ferguson and I had entered the night before. There was a second door, closer to me, and a third on the opposite side of the hall.

I looked into the office first, but it was empty. The other

room on that side of the hall was also deserted, a combination kitchen/dining room area furnished with a cheap dinette set. That left the door on the other side.

I opened the door carefully. There was no one inside there, either.

No one alive, that is.

It was a bedroom, with a dresser, a padded rocking chair, and a double bed. Ferguson was in the bed. I could see him in the light from the hall. He wouldn't be getting up anytime soon, not under his own power.

He lay on top of the spread, dressed exactly as he had been the last time I saw him. Maybe the shirt was different; it was hard to tell in the dim light that came in from the hall and the graying sky that I could see through the window.

There didn't seem to be much blood, but Ferguson hadn't died like Terry Shelton. He'd been shot. There were two holes in the front of his western shirt, one of them located right about in the center of his chest. There was blood around both holes, though not enough to stain the entire shirt. I walked over to the bed, reached out a finger, and touched one of the stains. It was still a little wet.

Ferguson lay there as if he'd been arranged, hands at his sides, legs straight out. His glasses were still on his face, but they looked slightly askew. Maybe he'd been shot somewhere else and placed on the bed. Maybe he'd been told to lie down and then he'd been shot. I didn't know, and I couldn't ask him.

Well, I could ask, but I didn't think he'd be able to come up with much in the way of an answer.

I looked at him for maybe a minute, and then I was out of there, using the tail of my sweatshirt to wipe the light switch and doorknobs I'd touched. I wiped the wall and the surface of the doors, too.

A minute later I was back in the Subaru, on the way to Galveston.

1 2

As THE SUBARU ROLLED down the freeway to Galveston, there was plenty of traffic headed in the opposite direction, all of it going toward the big city. It was not very long after sunrise, or what would have been sunrise if the day had been clear, but anyone who wanted to beat the really big crush had already started out, beginning a smaller crush of their own. Very few drivers were going toward Galveston, however, and my headlights played along the gray road in front of me without reflecting from the bumpers of any other cars.

I had a lot to think about. I turned on the car radio to see if it would help me. I found a station playing Smiley Lewis, who was singing the only really good version of "I Hear You Knockin'," but he didn't have any clues for me.

A confusing situation had now become even more confusing, not to mention more serious. It was bad enough to have one dead body in the case. Two were almost more than I cared to think about, especially since I still hadn't figured out how the first one fit in. I wondered if the undercover cop I'd talked to in The Sidepocket would remember me well enough to describe me. Probably. So would the bartender. But it didn't really matter as long as they never saw me again.

A man like Ferguson was bound to have plenty of enemies.

Of course if the cop recalled that I had mentioned Terry Shelton, and if someone in Houston had heard about the murder in Galveston, then things could get pretty interesting around my house. The odds of that happening, however, were small.

My greatest problem at the moment seemed to be that no matter what the Houston police were able to come up with *I* no longer had any suspects, except possibly Sharon Matthews, and no one knew were she could be found. I certainly didn't.

Hank Ballard and the Midnighters came on the radio singing "Let's Go, Let's Go, Let's Go." Great idea, Hank, but where the hell am I supposed to go? I thought about Sharon, going back over everything that had happened so far. There must have been something I'd overlooked, something that I hadn't thought about enough, something that would give me a crack to start poking around in.

Terry Shelton was dead.

Chuck Ferguson was dead.

Someone apparently wanted Dino dead.

I started to feel lucky that I'd only been beaten up.

The sky kept getting grayer, but that was it. There wasn't going to be any sun, not for a while if at all. Heavy, low clouds hung down, almost low enough to touch the roof of the Subaru. The Capris were singing "There's a Moon Out Tonight." Not here, there wasn't.

Something occurred to me just as the lead singer was stretching out that last "to-ooo-oo-oo-ni-iii-iight." Sharon had only recently found out about her mother's past. She hadn't been overjoyed by what she'd discovered. How might she have reacted, under the circumstances? Was it possible that she could have engineered her own kidnapping? She could have seen it as a way to make her father pay—if she'd known who her actual father was and not just what her mother had been. Even the shooting made a crazy kind of sense if you looked at it right. If she decided that she'd rather have a dead father than have his money. She'd been told that her father was dead, so she'd see to it that he *was* dead.

I thought about that angle. If I was right, Terry Shelton and Chuck Ferguson were mixed up in the plot somewhere. Why not? Sharon would need help to pull off something as complicated as a kidnapping.

So where did that leave me? Clyde McPhatter was asking "A Lover's Question," but I had a different kind of question in mind. I thought maybe I knew the answer now, or at least part of the answer. I sent the Subaru over the bridge and down toward Broadway just as a pink rim appeared on one of the clouds. Maybe the sun was going to shine after all.

Nameless was waiting for me when I got home. I stashed the pistol under the seat again, fed him, and changed sweatshirts. The bruises on my ribs looked like hell, but they didn't hurt as long as I didn't make any sudden moves.

While I was changing, I watched the early morning news from Houston. The remains of a young woman had been found in a field near La Marque. The sheriff was understandably agitated, since it was the fifth body that had been found in the same general area in less than a month. Someone very unpleasant was using the sheriff's county for a dumping ground. There wasn't really much left of the body, mostly scattered bones and a few scraps of clothing. The investigators estimated that the remains may have been in the field for as long as eight months. Maybe a year. Two gradeschoolers had found the remains late the previous afternoon when returning from a rabbit hunt.

I thought about Jan. I'd have to remember to call the sheriff's office and remind them to check her dental records. I'd sent them some time before, when the first body had been discovered. I didn't think this one was her, either, but I had to make sure.

Strangely enough, the reporter's story didn't bother me as much as it would have even a few days before. I was beginning to accept the fact that Jan might really be dead and that I was never going to find her, something that I had accepted intellectually a long time ago. It had never reached me emotionally, though, down in that dark cavern of the mind where we all really live. It reached me now, and my interest in Dino's problems had turned the trick.

Nameless had spread himself out on the couch, his back pressed against the cushions, his legs extended. He was nearly as long as the couch.

I picked him up and carried him down the stairs. "Sorry," I said, "but it's outside again." I tossed him out and went down the steps to the car. He sat and looked at me resentfully as I drove away.

I went by McDonald's for an Egg McMuffin and then drove down to the Bolivar ferry. I drove right by the street where Evelyn Matthews lived, but I noticed nothing out of the ordinary there.

At this time of day and year, there was no wait for the ferry. I drove right on the *Gib Gilchrist,* stopped the car, set the brake, and got out.

The ferry was far from full, but it began its journey anyway. There was a slight chop on the bay water, but nothing to make me uncomfortable. I get seasick very easily.

I hadn't brought any popcorn or stale bread to feed the seagulls, and neither had anyone else. This wasn't a tourist time of day. The gulls that followed us for a short distance, swooping and diving at the boat, soon gave up and went away. I looked for the dolphins that sometimes came to observe the ferry, but they were elsewhere, or maybe they were asleep. I didn't know what hours dolphins kept.

The trip took only about twenty minutes, and it wasn't until I drove off the boat that I remembered I hadn't found out Terry Shelton's address. It had occurred to me that

Shelton's house might be a good place to hide if you were Sharon Matthews and you wanted people to think you'd been kidnapped. It was free, after all, and there was really no reason for anyone to search there. Terry would have said that he hadn't seen her for several days if anyone had asked.

But no one was going to ask him because he was dead. Did Sharon know that? Would she still be there, if she had ever been? Had the police searched the house? It wouldn't take me long to answer at least one of those questions. The others might take a little longer.

I drove past the Bolivar Lighthouse. A hundred or more people had weathered the 1900 storm there. It didn't look any the worse for wear or for the ninety years that had passed. It stood as straight as ever, but it was safely out of the public's way behind a chain-link fence.

In the little town of Port Bolivar I stopped at a Stop-and-Go to ask about the Shelton house. The clerk was a woman about thirty-five, a little on the heavy side, wearing a striped uniform top. Her name tag said that she was "Debbie." I got a can of Big Red from the cooler and then paid her.

She gave me my change. "Thank you," she said. "Have a nice day."

I started to tell her that I had other plans, then thought better of it. No one wants to help out a smart aleck. "I'll try," I said. I started out the door and then turned back as if I'd just thought of something.

"Can I help you?" Debbie asked.

"Maybe so. I was just wondering. I heard the Shelton house was for sale."

"Oh, no, I don't think so," Debbie said. "You must've heard about something else. Wasn't it terrible about the Shelton boy, though?"

"What about him?" I took a sip of Big Red and looked guileless, or as close as I could come.

"Why he got killed over in Galveston. Got his neck

broke!" Debbie's eyes were wide with the horror of it.

"No kidding," I said.

"No kidding. Everybody wonders what it was all about." She looked around to see if any big-time drug dealers were listening. "I bet it was some kinda drug deal."

For an area that had once been known for bootlegging, drugs had become a new form of an old vice. "Probably," I said. "There's a lot of that going on. Well, I wouldn't want to buy a drug dealer's house."

Debbie shook her head. "I don't think it's for sale."

"I'm sure I heard it was. That big house just down the street from here, faces on the Intracoastal Waterway?"

"Well," she said, "it faces on the waterway, all right, but it's about half a mile up the road. It's yellow, with a green porch."

"Not the one I heard about, then," I said. I went on out the front glass doors, and tossed what was left of the Big Red, which was most of it, in the trash. Even for me, it was too early in the morning for Big Red.

I found the Shelton house without any trouble after that. I could see why Debbie thought Terry might have been involved with dope. The house was an ideal location. A boat could tie up at the dock, wait for a load of the stuff to arrive from Colombia, or wherever it was coming from these days, sail out into the Gulf to meet the ship, then sail back to the dock and unload into station wagons or vans that could carry the junk into Houston. It would work, if the Coast Guard didn't catch you. Since you'd have to sail right in front of the Coast Guard station, you'd have to have pretty good nerves, or very little sense. Money does strange things to people, though.

I stopped the car a few houses away from the Shelton place. It looked deserted, but I didn't feel like taking any chances. I didn't see anyone anywhere around, and for just a second I thought about slipping the pistol out from under the seat, but I didn't. This looked like a perfectly peaceful area, the kind of place where nothing ever happened and where kids played in the yards with their dogs.

I walked down to the house, which was raised up on posts about ten feet off the ground. There was a place underneath to park a car, but there wasn't one there. The curtains were drawn in all the rooms that I could see. There was no sign that the police had visited it, though I thought they probably had. And it was likely that Terry Shelton's parents had been there to look at his things. It would have been easy for Sharon to leave and return, of course. But if she had left, where had she gone?

I looked up at the house for a minute or two, then climbed the green stairs that led to the door. The door was not on the front of the house, but on the side. I knocked as if I were an insurance salesman or a poll taker. There was no answer.

I waited a second or two before I tried the doorknob. It didn't budge. I wondered if there was an alarm system. Well, there was one way to find out. I took a Visa card out of my billfold and slipped the latch. It didn't take more than a couple of seconds. The door opened easily. There was no deadbolt.

And no alarm. No bells rang, no buzzers buzzed, no lights flashed. Of course the phone could already be dialing the police station, but I didn't think that was likely. I eased into the cool dimness and shut the door behind me.

I stood quietly, waiting for my eyes to get used to the dim light. There was nothing exceptional to see when they did. A room with a couch, a bookcase, a TV set, a coffee table. A few magazines on the coffee table, *Time*, *Newsweek*, *National Geographic*. The subscription labels all had Terry's name on them. There was a carpet on the floor, but it didn't quite fit the size of the room. Probably bought as a remnant. There was no padding under it.

I was looking through the bookcase when I started getting

the feeling that I wasn't alone. Terry Shelton's taste in reading, or his parents', ran to paperbacks by writers like Stephen King and Robert R. McCammon. I had just flipped through a copy of McCammon's *They Thirst*, which was apparently about the vampire takeover of Los Angeles, when I began to suspect that someone was watching me.

I put the book back in place and turned around slowly. There were two doors leading out of the room I was in, and both probably led to bedrooms. The kitchen/eating area was a part of the room I was in, separated from the living section only by a long breakfast bar at which three stools stood.

I couldn't decide if there was someone in the room on the right or the one on the left. I wasn't even sure that there was anyone there at all. Maybe I was just reacting to the paperback I'd been looking at, with its bloody, toothy cover.

I stood and watched the doorways. There was no motion, no sound in the dimness behind them.

"Sharon?" I said. My voice cracked slightly, so I said it again. "Sharon?"

There was no answer. I walked to the door on the right, feeling like that character in "The Lady or the Tiger?" who has to choose between the doors. I could see a double bed, covered with a dark spread. There was a line of light on the floor at the bottom of the curtains.

"Sharon?" I said.

There was no answer, no sound of any kind. Feeling like a fool, I stepped through the doorway. I was convinced there was no one there.

Luckily my conviction didn't slow me down. I stepped pretty quickly and thereby avoided most of the blow that was aimed at me. It missed my head and hit me right between the shoulder blades. Even at that, I was flipped ass over elbows and landed on the bed.

My mind momentarily went into neutral and my body was paralyzed. Pain jabbed me in the ribs.

I got over my paralysis quickly and rolled to the side, which was just as well, since I managed to avoid the chair that came crashing down on the bed where I had been.

I slipped off the side of the bed onto the floor. I got my knees under me and raised my head up carefully, jerking it back down to avoid the chair once more. It was a black bentwood chair, very lightweight, but I had no desire for it to come into contact with my head no matter what it weighed. I wished sincerely and futilely that I had brought the Mauser, especially since the man wielding the chair was one of the gorillas from The Sidepocket's parking lot.

I didn't know what else to do, so I slid under the bed. It was dark and dusty under there, but I could look out and see the guy's feet. He was wearing a pair of white canvas deck shoes, and he was standing on the side of the bed opposite the one I'd slid off of, no doubt wondering what to do next.

He didn't know whether I was armed, but he was pretty sure I wasn't dangerous. After all, he'd taken me out once, with the help of his pals. As soon as he figured out where I was, he could toss the bed over and beat me to a pulp or just kneel down and shoot me if he had a pistol.

Maybe I could take him. I wasn't a small man by any means, and I was probably in good enough shape unless he kicked me in the knee, but there wasn't very much I could do in the uncomfortable position in which I found myself. I eased closer to the deck shoes, then reached out and grabbed the ankles sticking out of them. I jerked forward as hard as I could.

There was no rug on this floor, and as soon as the man's head came into contact with the floor I slithered out from under the bed and on top of him. He was surprised and stunned, but not out. He caught me under the chin with a forearm that snapped my head back and shivered my timbers.

Before I knew what was happening, he was up and aiming a kick at my head. I rolled away and tried to grab his foot, but I missed. I got a grip on his pants leg, but he jerked away.

Then the chair was coming at me again. He must have picked it up, though I don't remember seeing him do it. He didn't miss this time.

In the movies when someone gets hit with a chair, the chair splinters satisfactorily, and pieces of it fly all over the room. This was not a movie chair. It stayed in one piece, one leg hitting my head while the others hit my shoulders and ribs. I tried to get up, but I felt like the two-thousand-year-old man.

He swung the chair again. I somehow got my hands up and grabbed one of the legs. The man was so strong that he picked me the rest of the way up on the follow-through.

I was shaky, but I held on to the chair for all I was worth. Through all of this, neither of us had said a word. I was groaning and he was snorting, but that was it. Now I started yelling. Maybe someone would hear me and call the cops. I wasn't eager to be caught in Shelton's house, but it was better than being beaten to death with a bentwood chair.

We continued to struggle for the chair, with me yelling "Fire!" and "Murder!" and "Rape!" at the top of my lungs. I didn't really think anyone would rush to my aid, but maybe I could distract the gorilla.

He was far stronger than I was, but I wasn't about to let go of the chair. Then I noticed where we were. We had struggled away from the bed and were very close to the curtained windows.

I put everything I had into pulling the chair in my direction, my arms straining and burning with the effort. He had the top of the chair, and he applied an equal and opposite force. OK, more than equal.

Suddenly I relaxed, not only giving way but aiding him by leaning in his direction. He was surprised and went backward very quickly, stumbling when the back of his calves hit the low windowsill. I pushed as hard as I could then, and his back hit the curtain. The window shattered, and he went through it, still holding on to the chair. I had let it go. I didn't want it anymore.

I sat on the bed to catch my breath. When it was more or less back to normal, I walked over to the window and looked out. The curtains were hanging with their bottoms outside the sill now, and I pulled them back inside.

The ground in back of the house was not as low as it was in front, only about six feet from the windowsill. There was no one lying there. The chair lay harmlessly on the scruffy grass.

I locked the bedroom door. If he came after me again, he was going to have to kick it in, not that I thought he'd hesitate to do it. I sat on the bed and waited. Nothing happened for fifteen minutes. Maybe I'd hurt him at least a little.

I went into the bathroom and bathed my face. There was a lump forming on the left side of my head, just above the ear, but there were no other marks, though my ribs hadn't been improved any. I didn't even have a bloody nose.

While I was in the bathroom I looked around. There was a bottle of Old Spice, a can of Noxema shaving cream, half a package of Bic disposable razors, aspirin, a box of Puffs. A bar of Ivory soap on the rim of the tub. I went out, unlocked the bedroom door, and looked into the second bedroom. There was nothing unusual there, either.

Somehow, though, I was convinced that Sharon had been there, and I was equally certain that the guy who'd jumped me had been left there or sent there by someone just in case I happened by. I didn't know who he was or who had sent him, but I was more determined than ever to find out.

13

I T WAS GETTING ON toward late afternoon when I drove into the River Oaks section of Houston. My little Subaru looked as much out of place there as Dumbo at a mastodon convention. River Oaks was money, some of the million-dollar homes sitting boldly on their lots so that the underprivileged could drive by and see what they were missing, while other houses, just as expensive if not more so, were hidden behind high walls or dense foliage from the gawkers and shaded by the enormous expanses of trees that gave the area its name.

Jimmie Hargis lived in one of those houses. I doubted that his neighbors knew how he'd made his money, or cared, as long as he kept to himself, didn't bother anyone, and didn't try to attend their bridge parties, or whatever kind of parties people with that much money had. I'd never been invited to one anymore than Hargis had.

I drove down a tree-lined street to the address that Dino had given me and pulled off at a wrought-iron gate, painted black. An asphalt drive curved off into the trees, and I could see parts of the house through the limbs and foliage.

By the time I got my window rolled down, a voice was

123

speaking to me out of a metal speaker grille set in the stone gatepost. I gave my name, and thanks to a phone call that Dino had made earlier, the gate split down the middle and began to swing slowly inward. When it was open all the way, I drove through.

I parked in front of the house, an impressive Spanish-style number that appeared to sit on about half a block of expensive acreage. It was all white, with a red tile roof. There was black grillwork on all the windows. It would be a hard place to get into, or out of. There were frequent stories in the Houston papers about people who had died in fires in their homes, trapped by burglar bars as the flames raged through the dwellings. I figured that Hargis was safe enough. He could no doubt afford a good sprinkler system.

The front door was heavy wood, about the size of the front door of the Alamo. There was no knocker, but I didn't need one. By the time I got there, the door was already opening.

I have to admit that I was surprised by the man who stood there. He was a butler. There's no other way to describe him. He looked like a picture of Jeeves on the cover of a P. G. Wodehouse novel, starched white front and all. I'd read that there was a training school for real British butlers in Houston, but I'd never really given it much thought. Now I knew it was true. I expected him to say, "Right this way, sir."

He didn't, but what he did say was almost as good. "Come in, Mr. Smith. Mr. Hargis is expecting you."

I followed him down a tiled hallway. We must have looked like two players in a drawing-room comedy lost in a cathedral as we walked beneath the house's high, vaulted ceiling and beside its thick white walls.

Hargis met me in a room that I suppose he called his study. The butler stood aside, and I walked in. The walls were paneled in dark wood, and there was a thick wool carpet, also dark, on the floor. In the center of the room was a huge wooden desk, and the wall behind it was covered with bookshelves. Shiny leather-bound volumes crowded the shelves, as if Hargis had bought every reprint the Franklin Mint issued. I wouldn't be surprised if he had even read some of them.

Hargis stood behind the desk, looking nothing like I'd expected. From his reputation, I'd thought of him as being a large, tough-looking man. Instead, he was small and delicate, not over five four, with small bones; he couldn't have weighed over a hundred and ten. I'd never seen a picture of him, of course. He wasn't a man given to having his photo taken.

In the normal course of things Hargis would never have agreed to talk to me, much less to see me in his house. But this wasn't the normal course of things.

I'd gone by to see Dino after my little adventure on Bolivar and told him what happened. Now that the shock of being shot had worn off, he was feeling rotten, but he was alert enough to see that things were getting out of hand. Ferguson was dead, Sharon was still missing, Shelton was murdered, and someone had made a try at Dino. None of it made any sense, and the only link we had left to any of it was Hargis. Dino could pull enough strings to get him to talk to me. He'd arranged it by phone, called me, and here I was.

Hargis motioned me to a seat in one of the brown leather chairs in front of his desk, then sat down himself. His chair must have been custom-made, or maybe it just had a thick cushion in it. He looked to be taller than he was as he sat there, leaning slightly forward, his elbows on the desk, his arms crossed.

"Dino told me most of the story," Hargis said. He had a mellow, pleasantly modulated voice. "He did say that I should listen to you relate one other bit of the puzzle, however."

"I'm sure he told you about the three men who jumped me outside The Sidepocket," I said. "I can describe one of them pretty well. He's about thirty-five, at least six three, and weighs around two-fifty. Maybe he was a fighter once, or a football player. His nose has been broken a couple of times at least. Dark hair, wears a crew cut. Has a pretty bad scar on his forehead, above the right eye." I knew it was a bad one, or I wouldn't have been able to see it so well in the dim light of the room where we had fought.

Hargis sat and looked at me. He was wearing a gray pinstripe that must have set him back a thousand dollars, and a gold cuff link winked at me from one of its sleeves. How long had it been since I'd owned a shirt with French cuffs? I couldn't even remember. I felt a little shabby and cheap. I tried to compensate by feeling morally superior, but it didn't help much.

After a minute or so, Hargis began talking. "I agreed to talk to you, Mr. Smith, out of regard for an old relationship that Dino made a claim on. I must admit that I really do not see how any of this business affects me, or how it touches me in any way."

I started to tell him, but he raised a hand from the desk to silence me. "I'll be glad to hear your comments in a moment. For now, allow me to have my say. My connection with Chuck Ferguson is purely a business one. He was the manager of one of my clubs, and that was all. It was not a particularly profitable club, though I must say that business improved slightly when Ferguson took over. It was his idea to convert it from a topless club to a place where local bands of dubious ability could display their talents, such as they are. Certainly the new attractions caused much less trouble with the city.

"At any rate, it developed into a fairly successful club, but it still wasn't among my top investments. So when Ferguson came to me with the idea of buying it, I listened with interest. He had knocked about a bit in the club business, and I believe that he'd done other kinds of work earlier in his career, though I never questioned him about that. He wanted a place of his own, a place where he could make a little money and feel as if he belonged. It didn't seem too much to ask, and since I had no real desire to keep The Sidepocket, I sold it to him."

Once again I started to interrupt, and once again he held up a palm. "Please. Let me tell this. I was not at all sure of how Ferguson intended to get the money to pay me, but he insisted that he could get it and that he could pay me in cash." Hargis allowed himself a thin smile. "For a man of my profession and inclinations, cash has a certain appeal. And I am not a man to question another's sources of revenue. Eventually we agreed on a price, and Ferguson asked for a short time to get the money. The papers were taken care of, and Ferguson came through with the money." He smiled again. "People rarely try to cheat me in money matters, Mr. Smith. I did not ask where he got it.

"Now, as for the . . . ah . . . individual you have described. I must confess that in my profession I have from time to time been forced to hire men to do jobs that require a certain amount of strength and daring."

I thought he had a nice way of putting things, but I didn't try to interrupt again.

"Often I do not see these individuals myself, as they are contracted for by others, and I can say with a fair amount of certainty that I have never seen the person you describe. That does not mean that he has never worked under my employ, but it is very unlikely that he is working for me at the present time."

He paused, and I thought that maybe it was my turn to talk, but I waited a few more seconds. Which was just as well.

"Now, Mr. Smith, you see that I have spoken quite frankly to you. Much more frankly than I would have done under ordinary circumstances. But these are not ordinary circumstances. The police have visited me today. I am not fond of being visited by the police."

"Me either," I said. I couldn't resist, and he didn't seem to mind. But that was probably because he paid me absolutely no attention at all.

"Ferguson's murder is causing me trouble," he said. "Trouble that I wish to avoid."

Someone had found the body then. "I didn't report it," I said.

"I didn't mean to imply that you did," he said impatiently. At least he had heard me that time. "The point is that the city is on one of its periodic crusades to regulate businesses of the sort in which I have an interest. Any scandal connected to me at this time is most irritating and inconvenient. I certainly had nothing to do with either Ferguson's death or the attack on Dino. But I would very much like to know who did. I would like to know even before the police find out, if that could be arranged, though it is not entirely necessary."

He wasn't smiling now, and as I looked at his cold eyes I could see why he was sitting on his side of the desk and I was on the other, why he owned a house in River Oaks and I was a house-sitter in Galveston. Why he had on an expensive suit and a shirt with French cuffs and I was wearing a sweatshirt and jeans.

"I know that I have not been able to help you much, except in a negative way," he said. "But I feel that the information that I am requesting would be fair trade for the time I've given you here today."

"I appreciate the time," I said. "And I appreciate your being frank with me. I hope you won't mind if I ask just one indelicate question, since you've assured me that you had nothing at all to do with any of this."

He gave me a straight look, which he might not have meant to be unfriendly. "Only one?" he said.

"Only one. Since you aren't involved at all, did you ever

hear of any plot against Dino or to kidnap the girl? Sharon Matthews."

He leaned back in his chair. "I suppose that might be interpreted as a bit indelicate if the answer were yes, but the answer is no. I assure you that I have no knowledge of anything relating to the kidnapping of Sharon Matthews other than what you and Dino have told me today."

"All right," I said. "I believe you. But before I agree to tell you anything else I find out, I want you to agree to help me with something."

He raised one eyebrow. The left one. I never could understand how someone could do that. "What?"

I told him about Jan. "If you ever hear anything, anything at all, that might connect to her—"

"I'll be glad to let you know," he said. "It's quite unlikely, however."

"I know," I said.

I was hungry by the time I got back to the Island, but I didn't take the time to eat. I was looking for another source of information, the only one I had any confidence in aside from Sally West. It was a fairly nice night, not too cool, and I found him almost immediately, dumpster diving behind a huge Kroger supermarket on Sixty-first Street.

At least I thought it was him. All I could see were legs hanging out of the dumpster. I drove the Subaru down to the end of the buildings, parked, and walked back.

"That you in there, Harry?" I said.

There was a noise of papers rustling and then a hollow banging as something hit one of the sides of the dumpster. Then a burlap bag hit the pavement beside me. God knows what was in it. Harry followed it down.

"You're looking sharp, Harry," I said.

In the light of the blue mercury vapor lamp that flooded the area I could see that he was wearing at least two shirts, one black and red flannel and one underneath, which was some unidentifiable miracle fabric. Over them both he wore a ripped jacket of olive drab with the lining showing through a couple of the jagged holes in the sides. He had on a pair of olive drab pants that hit him about halfway up the calves. A pair of faded jeans underneath extended a little farther down.

"That you, Tru?" he said. "You look like you doin' all right for youself. Want a bite to eat?" He reached for the sack.

"No, thanks," I said, maybe too quickly for politeness.

He reached into the sack and came out with what appeared to be a very dented, labelless can of dog food or cat food. The can was the right shape, and I was willing to bet it wasn't tuna.

"This go pretty good 'bout now," he said.

I took a step back. "My God, Harry. How can you eat that stuff."

He looked at me, amazed that I would ask such a stupid question. "You jus' takes a piece of bread," he said, extending one hand as if it held the slice he was speaking of, "and you jus' spreads it on." He made a spreading motion with the hand that held the can.

I'd met Harry—"Outside" Harry, most people called him—when I was looking for Jan. I'd had occasion to visit a few alleyways, and Harry had been in more than one of them. I'd struck up a conversation one day, more out of curiosity than anything else, and soon discovered that he was a mine of information. No one knew how old he was, but I'd talked to people who swore that he must be at least eighty. He'd been on the Island for as long as anyone could remember. After so many years, no one really paid any attention to him. He came and went, picking the garbage for whatever he needed or wanted. During all that time, he'd heard and seen a lot and remembered most of it. Despite what many people thought, he wasn't feebleminded. He was just old.

"I think I'll skip the meal tonight," I said.

"Got me a head of lettuce in here, too," he said, reaching back into the sack. "Couple oranges, too."

"Save them for yourself, Harry. I'm not hungry." It wasn't much of a lie. Thinking about Harry's diet took away my appetite.

Harry twisted the top of his bag shut. "Well, I jus' like to share. But if you don't want none . . ." He looked up at me sharply. "Must want somethin', though."

"Just to talk."

"Well, tha's all right, but I got to work." Harry shuffled off toward the next dumpster. "Some folks got to stay busy."

I followed along after him. "I wondered if you'd seen a man," I said.

Harry stopped. "Seen lotsa men," he said. "See 'em all the time."

"This is a particular man." I described the man I'd previously described to Jimmie Hargis.

Harry listened carefully, his head cocked to one side. He was short to begin with, and with his bag tossed over his shoulder he looked like a black gnome standing in the blue light. "Might've seen that one," he said. He turned and shuffled off again.

I went after him. This was the way conversations with Harry were usually carried on.

He stopped at a brown-painted dumpster, tossed his bag in, then pulled himself over the rim. He dug around for a while with his legs sticking out. I could hear him tossing things around. Then his legs disappeared inside. I hoped I was half as agile as he was when I reached his age.

A cardboard box flew out of the dumpster and hit the ground beside me. Then Harry's head appeared above the rim. "Prob'ly around Corea's, somewhere in there," he said. The head disappeared.

"Thanks, Harry," I said.

I walked back to the Subaru and took out the six-pack of Old Milwaukee I'd bought earlier. I carried it back to the dumpster and set it down where Harry would be sure to find it. I'd tried giving him money a time or two, but he was always insulted by the offer. He was self-sufficient and proud of it. He'd once complained, though, that he never found any beer in the dumpsters. Since then I'd left a few six-packs lying around. He was amazed at the turn in his fortunes.

I never asked him how beer went with cat food.

I didn't really want to know.

1 4

"I HAVEN'T SMOKED at all since Dino got here," Evelyn Matthews told me when I noted the absence of ashtrays in her living room. "It bothers Dino, and I've wanted to quit for years."

"I guess Dino's as good an excuse as any to get started on a health kick," I said.

"Better than no excuse at all." She walked me back to the room where Dino was propped up on the bed. He didn't look any better than he had the last time I'd seen him, but then he didn't look any worse. He smiled when he saw Evelyn.

"I take it you don't have any complaints about the nursing," I said.

"Not a one," he said. "Tell me what you found out."

I told him. It didn't amount to much.

"I didn't figure Hargis to be in on something like this," he said. "There's no reason for him to be trying to get rid of me. Besides, the money is just small potatoes to him. Where's this Corea's place you mentioned?"

"It's a little mom-and-pop grocery just off Broadway," I said. "Outside Harry knows alleys behind all the places like that, and sometimes he knows who goes in and out the fronts."

Dino's forehead wrinkled. "That little place not too far from my house? Some kinda stucco on the outside, painted beige?"

"That's the place."

"Puts the guy kinda close to home," he said. "Think he was watching my house?"

"Who knows? I thought I'd check around the neighborhood tomorrow and see if I could find out anything."

"I guess it's worth a try. You talk to Ray today?"

I was surprised that he'd asked. "'What Ray doesn't know, Ray can't tell,'" I said.

"Yeah, well, I expect he's pretty worried by now. I think you better go by and check on him. Make sure he hasn't called the cops in on this, not that he would. Let him know what's going on."

"OK."

"And for God's sake, Tru, try to make some sense of this, will you?"

"Sure," I said. I was willing to try. I just didn't know how.

The lights were on in Dino's house, and Ray came to the door. He didn't seem especially surprised to see me.

"What's happening, Tru?" he said.

"Not much."

We went into the living room. The huge television set was blaring away, but it wasn't tuned to any station I'd seen Dino watching. As best I could make out, three men wearing space helmets and gauzy white outfits were chasing a girl wearing a stainless steel bikini through a huge swamp of mangrove trees and shallow water. An alligator rested on a log that pushed its way out of the thick mist rising from the water.

"MTV," Ray said. He walked over to the couch, located the remote, and clicked the set off. There was a drink sitting on the coffee table, and he picked it up. "Big Red?" he said.

"No thanks. I just wanted to stop by and see how the payoff went last night."

"I don't know," Ray said. He swirled the ice cubes around in his drink. "Dino hasn't been back since he sent me away."

"Does that worry you?"

He took a nip from his drink. "Not a bit. Dino knows how to take care of himself. He's been doing it for a long time. He'll turn up."

"I thought you took care of him."

Ray smiled. "Man, all I do is bring the drinks."

"Any more calls?"

"No more. I guess they got what they wanted."

"I guess so," I said, but of course I knew they hadn't.

I didn't feel a bit bad about not letting Ray in on the whole story. If he wasn't worried, there was no need to tell him anything. Dino's first thought had been right. If he didn't know, he couldn't tell.

When I got home I sat down and went over what I knew. I thought at first about calling Vicky, but I was too tired, not having slept much the night before and having had a pretty busy day up to that point.

I still believed that Sharon Matthews had in some way engineered her own disappearance, possibly with the help of Chuck Ferguson. I thought that she'd stayed at Terry Shelton's place for at least part of the time she'd been gone. But I couldn't for the life of me figure out why Ferguson and Shelton were dead, much less who had killed them.

Unless.

Unless Ferguson had hired the three goons, and they had decided to cut him and Shelton out and get all the money for themselves. It made a crazy kind of sense. If they killed Dino, then all they had to do was pick up the money and run. No one would come after them, except Ferguson, who would want his cut. So they killed him too.

That scenario didn't bode too well for Sharon. They could have killed her already if it was accurate. Maybe it wasn't, though. I just didn't know.

I fed Nameless, who had a notion that he wanted to stay inside for a while. I suppose that I'd been neglecting him for the past few days, but I tossed him out anyway. I was hoping to get some sleep, and I didn't need him jumping up in the bed with me and demanding to be put out after I dozed off. He refused even to look back at me as he stalked off into the darkness.

I slept, but not well. I dreamed of Jan when we were kids. There was a swing in our backyard, and I was pushing her. She was wearing a blue dress. Soon I was pushing her so high that when I looked at her she was framed against the sky. Because of the blue dress and the blue sky, I could hardly see her. I could see only her face, arms, and legs. Then she fell out of the swing. I ran under her to catch her, but I couldn't see her at all now. She had disappeared into the blueness. I could hear her screaming, but I couldn't see her. And then the dream started all over again. It repeated itself over and over like a tape loop.

I dreamed of Dino, too, and Ray. Dino was sitting on the porch of his large white plantation house in a white wicker chair. He was dressed like Rhett Butler, and Ray was serving him a mint julep on a crystal tray. "Yas, suh," Ray said. "Ah jus' brangs the dranks."

When I finally woke up, I felt like I'd run the Boston Marathon. Maybe I was better off on the nights I didn't sleep at all. I thought about going to the seawall for a run, but the knee was still tender. No need to push it. The fight the day before hadn't helped it any.

It was still too early to do much of anything else, though, so I read a few pages in the Faulkner book and then went down and let Nameless in. He ate a whole package of Tender Vittles and whined for more, but I wouldn't give in. He gave me a look that indicated how much our relationship had deteriorated and marched upstairs, tail held high.

I followed him up, read a few more pages, and got dressed. By that time, Nameless had made himself comfortable in the middle of my bed, and I had to roust him out to make it up. He dug his claws into the bedspread, pulling it halfway off the bed before he let go.

"You can be replaced, you know," I said, but he ignored me. As I carried him downstairs, I found myself wondering if Vicky liked cats. Some people were allergic to them. I'd have to ask her.

By the time I'd eaten an Egg McMuffin at my favorite restaurant, it was eight-thirty, not too early to visit Corea's Market. I dove over and went in. It wasn't exactly Apple Tree. The stock was scanty and the light was bad. As far as I could tell, though, it was clean.

There was a Formica-topped counter to the right of the door. An old wooden-bodied cash register sat on the counter, and there was a chubby old man standing behind it. He had thinning gray hair and wore a pair of half-glasses. He was wearing a white apron that tied behind his back, a khaki-colored shirt, and matching pants.

There was only one customer in the store, a stooped old lady wearing a long skirt and a shawl. Her skirt was so long I couldn't see her feet. She was standing at one of the shelves that lined the walls, looking very carefully at a can of something or other. She held the can so close to her face her nose was nearly touching it. I wondered why the man in the apron didn't get some better lighting, or at least let her borrow his glasses.

I stood in the doorway for a second or two, then walked to the counter.

"Can I help you?" the man said. His voice was firm and young; it didn't go with the gray hair and the wrinkles that I could now see on his face.

"I'm looking for someone," I said. "I heard he comes in here now and then."

"And who might that be?"

I described the man with whom I'd had the fight. The old man listened politely, meanwhile keeping a sharp eye on the old woman in the shawl.

"I think I've seen a man like that," he said when I finished. "He hasn't been in for a few days, though."

"What does he buy?"

"A little of everything. He's been a good customer. Buys a big bill every time he comes in. I hope he's not in some kind of trouble."

"No," I said. "He just owes me money."

"Well, he ought to be able to pay you. Buys a big bill, like I said, and he always pays in cash."

"Thanks," I said, and went back outside. If the guy was shopping there, he must be staying close by. And if he was buying a lot, he was probably buying for more people than just himself. Not that he wasn't perfectly capable of eating quite a bit, a man his size.

I strolled around the neighborhood of mostly rundown houses. There were some beautiful old homes on the Island, but there were a lot of the other kind, too. Unpainted frames, dilapidated fences, yards beaten down to the bare dirt or choked with weeds and brush. It didn't take long to find the one I was looking for, the one with the sign in front that said ROOMS FOR RENT.

I walked up on the sagging porch and rapped on the door. In a minute or so it was opened by a woman wearing a dress that sagged over her body like a limp tent. Her face was brown and wrinkled, and her dark hair was streaked with gray.

"Joo wan' a room?" she said in a thick Hispanic accent.

"Looking for a friend." I described the man again.

She thought about it, but she decided that I wasn't posing any kind of threat. "He stay here, si. But no longer." She started to close the door.

"Wait!" I said. "When did he leave."

She looked at me again. "A day. Two days." She moved the door.

I grabbed the edge of the door and held it. "Did he say where he was going?"

"No. Ees not my business. He pay, he go. Say nothing."

I released the door and watched it close. The woman was probably telling the truth. These weren't the kind of fellows to leave a forwarding address with the landlady. I stood on the porch and looked around. I was hardly more than six blocks from Dino's house. They must have been watching him all the time.

I walked back to the grocery store. There didn't seem to be much else I could do there, so I got in the car and drove away.

It was a pleasant day, not sunny, but mild. I drove on down to The Strand, where business still wasn't booming. There were a few tourists about, but not the numbers that the merchants really wanted to see. I parked the car and walked to the shop where Vicky worked. I noticed that the place next door, where Terry Shelton had been killed, was locked up. A blue-bordered sign hanging on one of the glass doors read CLOSED.

Vicky was behind the counter of the soap store, but she wasn't wearing her pink workout suit. Today's was blue. Her hair was caught up in a ponytail. I was surprised at how glad I was to see her. I'd hardly thought of women in the year I'd been looking for Jan.

She looked up when I walked in the door, and if I was any judge of smiles she was glad to see me, too.

"When's lunch hour?" I asked.

She looked at her watch, a white plastic case on a white plastic band. "Any minute now. Why?"

"I thought we might go over to Hill's and eat. Can you get away?"

"I haven't sold any soap all week. Sure I can get away. But I really should wait until the official lunch hour."

"So wait. I'll wait with you." There was a wicker chair in a front corner of the shop near the window. I went and sat in it. "I'll be all right if I'm not overcome by the perfume." The smell of all that soap was powerful. I wondered if Vicky had ever gotten used to it.

"Well, it won't be long," she said. "You can stand it."

"Yeah," I said. "I'm a tough guy."

She puttered around the shop for a while, reaching in the counter to arrange soap that looked arranged already. Then she said, "I've been thinking about your sister."

"In what way?" I said.

"Oh, I just wondered if she'd ever been in the shop, if maybe I'd ever seen her." She walked around the counter and came to stand by the window. "It must really hurt, not knowing."

"Not as much now," I said. "It did at first. A lot."

"You blamed yourself," she said. It was just a statement, flat, unemotional. There wasn't any doubt in it.

"You could tell that?"

"I could tell. Just by the way you talked about it." She looked down at me. "But you weren't to blame at all."

"I know that," I said. "It just took me a long time to admit it."

She smiled. "I'm glad you admitted it, then."

"This other case helped."

"Terry?"

"Yeah."

A woman came in then and actually bought a few bars of soap. When I heard Vicky tell her how much she owed, I thought I knew why soap hadn't been selling so well.

Vicky rang up the sale, then came back over to stand by my chair. "The shop next door's been closed ever since Terry was killed."

"I saw the sign," I said.

"Have you found out anything yet about who did it?"

"No. I actually haven't found out much of anything."

She didn't press me, which was just as well. I couldn't have told her any more. After a few minutes we walked over to Hill's to eat.

This Hill's wasn't the original Hill's, which had been on Seawall Boulevard. This one was located just across a street and a parking lot from the shop, on Pier Nineteen. The shrimp fleet was anchored all around, and the air was heavy with a powerful fishy smell. The mound of oyster shells around the restaurant may have had something to do with it.

We both had a bowl of gumbo, to which I added a dollop of Tabasco sauce. Vicky didn't. We made small talk, and then I thought to ask if the man I'd been looking for had ever been around Terry's shop.

"He sounds familiar," Vicky said. "Really big? Wide shoulders."

"That's the one." I crumpled the cellophane that I'd finally been able to remove from a package of four crackers. It crackled in my fingers.

"I think I might have seen him more than once," she said. "I think he went to the shop a couple of times, at least. He was a hard man to miss."

"What about the day Terry was killed?"

"I don't think so, but then I didn't see anyone go in. And somebody must have been there."

"It wasn't me. You know that."

"Yes," she said.

"It makes me wonder, though," I said, "how the police investigation is coming along."

"They came back to the shop once. Yesterday. They just asked me if anyone had been by looking for Terry, things like that."

"You didn't mention me, I hope."

She smiled. "No. I didn't think you'd like that."

She was right. It sounded as if the police were just as much in the dark as I was. I wasn't going to help them out any, not yet. Besides, I didn't know how much good the description would be to them. It was interesting to know that the man had been in the shop where Terry died, but knowing it didn't prove anything.

I explained my theory about the case to Vicky as we walked back to the soap store.

"You mean you think she kidnapped herself?" she said.

"Similar things have happened before. I'm just trying to figure out how the big guy and Terry come into it." I hadn't told her the rest of the story, about Dino's attempt to deliver the money and about Ferguson's murder.

"Maybe they were helping her, giving her a place to hide," Vicky said.

"That's what I thought, what I still think. But why was Terry killed? That part of it doesn't fit."

Vicky couldn't figure it any better than I could. I left her at the store and told her that I would call. I thought I'd come to a dead end, so I went to see Dino and tell him.

"They've called again," Evelyn said when she opened the door.

1 5

THERE ARE A FEW things I like to think I do well, but waiting is not one of them. I didn't have much choice, however, since the call had been very clear about the time. Once again, the small hours of the morning had been chosen, but this time the place was different. An abandoned warehouse near the Southern Pacific tracks just off Port Industrial Boulevard, exactly one mile from the Pelican Island Causeway, at 2 A.M.

"I hope you asked how you could trust them," I told Dino.

"Damn right, I did. They said they'd made a mistake, weren't sure that it was really me in the car. One of their guys got trigger-happy, they said. He won't be there this time. They said." He was propped up on the bed with fresh white bandages around him. He didn't really look fit enough to be delivering a ransom.

"Did they know you'd been hit?"

"They didn't say anything about it, so neither did I. I'll be there."

"So will I," I said.

"And I will, too," Evelyn said. "I'm driving."

I didn't try to argue.

That was about twelve hours from the time the drop was to be made. I had plenty of time to do some planning. "Are they going to have Sharon with them?"

"So they say," Dino told me. "I don't think I believe it."

"Me neither," I said. "But then I'm not sure what to believe about all this anymore. If you don't believe them, why take the chance?"

"Because they might be telling the truth."

I didn't say anything. It wasn't my daughter, and I wasn't the one trying to make up for whatever it was that I'd left undone, not this time. But I knew the feeling.

"I'm going to be there a long time before you," I said. "You think they trust *you*?"

"I guess they do. Nothing was said about the police this time. They must think I'm dumb enough to come alone again."

"Well, you are. At least as far as they'll ever find out from seeing the car. Evelyn can drive you. I'll be arriving a little early."

"How early might that be?"

"As soon as I can get there," I said.

Evelyn went back into the living room, where she made a beeline for a pack of cigarettes that was lying on the little TV set.

"I can't help it," she said, looking at me as she lit up. Her dark eyes were sunken. "I tried."

I smiled. "I don't blame you. I almost want one myself."

She held out the pack.

"No thanks." I glanced back at the bedroom. "What do you think?"

"He can make it. He's tough. That's one thing I've learned in the last couple of days. When I was trying to get him in the car? He was bleeding, and I knew he was hurt. I thought he might be dying. But he never said a thing, except 'Get us out of here.' "

She didn't have to tell me that Dino was tough. My knee could testify to that. So could plenty of other people. Even in high school he was a terror. Everyone hated to scrimmage against him because he couldn't seem to get the idea that we were only practicing. He flattened everyone who came his way. No exceptions. No one could hit him hard enough or often enough to keep him down. Not for long.

"He's tough, all right," I said.

"I think the only thing that bothers him is that I don't have a TV in the bedroom," Evelyn said, waving her left hand at a plume of smoke that lingered in front of her face. "He makes me watch the soaps and tell him what's going on."

"Move the TV," I said. "I'll help you."

"Maybe tomorrow."

I went to one of the platform rockers and sat down. "Tell me more about Sharon," I said.

"More? Like what?"

"I don't know, really. Is she strong-minded. Rebellious?"

Evelyn got an ashtray out of a cabinet in the kitchen and sat down in the other rocker. "I don't know what you mean. Or what you're really asking." She stubbed out her cigarette.

"What I'm really asking is whether you think your daughter would kidnap herself."

I give her credit. She didn't appear shocked and didn't try to tell me that I was crazy. She actually thought about it. "I don't think so," she said finally. "Why?"

"Resentment. I mean, she found out not just that you were a prostitute"—somehow I couldn't bring myself to use the word *whore* to her anymore—"but also that Dino was her father. One of the richest men on the Island, and he never said a word to her. Never acknowledged that she was alive. Not that you were any help. Your pride, or whatever it was that kept you from asking for anything, didn't make things any easier."

She lit another cigarette. "I guess it didn't. I'm sure it was a mistake, now. Dino isn't what I thought he was."

I eased off a bit. "Maybe he was, at one time. Twenty years of watching daytime TV can change a man."

She laughed. "Sharon *is* strong-willed," she said, to change the subject or to get back to what we were originally talking about. "I remember when she was a baby, before she could even walk, I had to keep her from pulling the pans out of the cabinets in the kitchen. One day after I'd stopped her at least three times, and then a fourth, she banged her head on the floor in frustration. She had a terrible bruise. I thought the neighbors would turn me in for child abuse."

"Then you think it's possible?"

"That she's behind all this? I suppose so, but it just doesn't seem likely. I've never given her cause for something like this."

"But you never told her about Dino. You never told her about your past."

She looked down. "It didn't seem to matter."

"Things like that never do," I said. "Not until it's too late."

When I left Evelyn's house, there was still a lot of time until 2 A.M. I drove by and fed Nameless, who ate only enough to keep himself from starving by the next time I came home. He certainly wouldn't deign to eat enough to acknowledge any degree of dependence on me.

There was nothing in the house that I wanted to eat, so I dropped by a Stop-and-Go and picked up some Slim Jims and a couple of sixteen-ounce bottles of Big Red. The Big Red would be warm before I got a chance to drink it, but I would just have to suffer.

Pelican Island, a very small island next to Galveston, must have seemed like a great idea to developers at one time, but it hadn't panned out. The expected boom had never oc-curred. Instead, all that occupied the island were the Seawolf

Park, featuring a real World War II submarine, and the campus of Texas A&M's Galveston branch. The causeway was certainly nice, though.

I drove down Fifty-first Street, but I didn't use the causeway other than to get my bearings from it. I checked my speedometer so that I'd know when I'd driven a mile and turned left down Port Industrial Boulevard, which ran alongside the ship channel. At the edge of the channel I could see a huge square mountain of sulfur, bigger than my house. It was being chewed away and loaded on a ship.

It was good to see the activity. There wasn't that much work for longshoremen in Galveston anymore. Some who had been living there for years were considering moving away to find jobs. The union wasn't painting a rosy picture of the future, either.

I easily found the warehouse I was looking for, but I didn't stop the car. I drove on by and waited until I found a side street where a couple of other cars were parked. I pulled in behind one of them and left the Subaru there. I walked back to the warehouse, carrying my sack of Slim Jims and Big Red. The Mauser was stuck in my waistband, covered by the sweatshirt. There was no one around to see me.

The warehouse stood on a block by itself, surrounded by what had once been a graveled parking lot. There hadn't been any traffic in the lot for a long time; it had sprouted weeds and grass, and weeds grew thick around the base of the building itself.

I stood in an alley a block away and checked out the warehouse. It was a tin building, built up off the ground so that trucks could back right up for loading or unloading. On the side that I could see, there were three sliding doors, all covered with tin, that could be opened from inside.

I went closer, and I could see that there was a double wooden door in one end, reached by steps leading up to a small porch. I circled around the building and saw three more sliding doors on the side opposite the others.

I could almost feel the emptiness of the building. There was such a stillness about it that it would have been almost impossible for anyone to be inside. The tin was weathered and gray, peeling away in places from the frame, which appeared to be made of the same huge timbers that buttressed the edges of the floor that I could see below the doors. These timbers were chipped and shredded by the bumpers and tailgates of the trucks that had backed into them and used them for cushioning for a good many years. In a couple of places around the bottom of the building, the tin was missing completely, but I could see nothing in the darkness underneath.

I hadn't really expected anyone to be there, but I watched for an hour anyway, holding on to my sack and moving from place to place. An occasional car passed by, but never the same one twice. No one appeared to be interested in me. Finally, I went inside.

Or underneath, to be more exact. The floor was so high that I really didn't even have to bend double to slip beneath the timber at one of the places where the tin was missing. I stood for a few minutes, letting my eyes adjust to the darkness. Eventually I could see that there were huge pilings holding up the flooring. I had hoped to find a break, a missing timber, but there was none. I couldn't do any good under there, or I didn't think I could. So I lurked around until there were no cars coming and then came out and hopped up on one of the timbers jutting out from the sides. There was a powerful twinge from my knee to remind me that what I was doing probably was not just going to be a picnic with Slim Jims and soft drinks.

I stood up and tried to slide one of the doors, but it wouldn't move. There was no place to get a real grip, since the framing was all inside the building. Then I pushed hard at the bottom, which swung inward. I pushed even harder and made a space big enough for me to slip through.

It was dark and dusty inside. There were gaps in the tin roof, so a little light got through. Dust motes spun in the stray beams of the late afternoon sun. I looked around. There were a few cardboard cartons in one corner. Their sides were collapsed and broken. A couple of empty Pennzoil cans lay beside them, triangular holes punched in the tops.

There were four heavy posts supporting the roof. A calendar on one of them advertised FRED'S AUTO SUPPLY. The date was 1984. A faded picture showed a well-developed young woman with red hair, who was holding a wrench in one hand and a gigantic sparkplug in the other. She was wearing a very small and tight pair of overalls.

I walked down to the double doors that opened onto the porch. They opened easily, and I felt a bit foolish. I should have tried the front entrance. To my right was a dilapidated platform scale. Three thick iron weights used for balance sat on top of the arm.

Built into the corner of the warehouse was a rest room. I looked in. I've seen dirty rest rooms before, but this one was a prizewinner. The toilet might have been made of black enamel, except that a few streaks of yellowish white showed through. Most of the white paint had worn off the seat so that gray wood showed. Even the lavatory was filthy. Whoever had worked here hadn't possessed a strong sense of personal hygiene. Even allowing for the fact that the building had been vacant for years, the place was a mess. It looked as if it had been used for a century without being cleaned.

There was one good thing about the bathroom, from my point of view. It obviously had been added to the building sometime after the original construction had been completed, and instead of extending the walls up to the high tin roof, the builder had made them eight feet high and had even put in a ceiling. I hoped the ceiling was sturdy enough to hold me.

I pushed the scale over so that I could stand on the arm, and with a little scrabbling, holding my sack between my teeth, I got up. My knee was throbbing, but after I rested for a minute it was fine.

There were a few boxes up there, filled with stuff that whoever had once owned the building had by now long forgotten: rolls of adding machine paper, stacks of invoices held together by string and crumbling rubber bands, and some grayish-green ledger books. Everything was covered with a thick layer of dirt and dust.

I shoved the boxes as close to the edge as I could. I could sit behind them and relax as much as it was possible to do under the circumstances. I'm not allergic to dust, but it filled my nostrils and made me want to sneeze.

To take my mind off things, I ate a couple of Slim Jims and drank a Big Red. I felt better, knowing that I wouldn't starve or die of thirst while I was waiting. After an hour, however, sitting on the boards began to make me sore. I shifted position as often as I could without making too much noise.

A lot of things can go through your mind when you're waiting like that, waiting for something to happen and not knowing exactly what you're waiting for. I thought about Dino and Ray and the old days, the times we had. I thought about Jan. I thought about Evelyn Matthews and her daughter.

For the first time, I wondered whether Evelyn could possibly be involved in the kidnapping. What if it was her resentment, rather than her daughter's, that had led to a desire for revenge against Dino? What if she had told Sharon about Dino and his part in her past? What if the two of them had cooked up the kidnapping between them?

I convinced myself that it wasn't possible. If she had been in on things, Evelyn would simply have let Dino be killed at the airport rather than save him. She could have had both the money and her revenge, easily enough. No, it had to be Sharon.

I sat there and constructed a new theory. Or revised the old one. Sharon and Terry had gone to Chuck Ferguson for help. He'd found the three bruisers through his contacts with the Houston underworld. It wouldn't be hard for him to find three men like that. He'd hired them, but they'd gotten greedy and begun eliminating the other participants in the scheme, starting with Shelton. Maybe Sharon had managed to escape them, but they still had Dino's name. So they decided simply to kill him and make off with the money. For that matter, maybe Sharon was already dead, buried somewhere on Bolivar. She wouldn't be the first person buried over there. Since they couldn't produce her, they had to kill Dino to get the money.

It all sounded highly plausible while I was lying there in the dusty dark of the abandoned warehouse. I had a feeling that it wouldn't sound that way to me in the cold light of the outside. There had to be something I was missing, something that would clear everything up and bring it into focus. All I had to do was think of that one thing, and all would become clear. But I couldn't think of it.

The time dragged by. Every time I punched the light button on my watch to check, five seconds would have rolled by.

About eight o'clock I had another Big Red, and about five minutes later I realized that a major disadvantage of being where I was included the fact that the toilet facilities were separated from me by the ceiling. I didn't want to climb down, but I didn't want to use the Big Red bottle, either.

So I went down. There was no water in the toilet, but that didn't matter. I pulled the decrepit door closed after I finished and climbed back up.

Another hour or so passed, dragging by like a snake with a broken back. There was very little traffic outside. I amused myself by timing the passing cars, but I quit after three. The first interval was ten minutes; the next, fourteen.

Finally I pulled a couple of ledgers from one of the boxes

and used them like a pillow, lying on my back on the board ceiling. I would make a lousy fakir, but I tried to clear my mind and relax.

Eventually, I did.

16

THEY CAME AROUND MIDNIGHT. It was very dark in the warehouse, and I didn't want to risk even the light from my watch, but midnight was about right.

I had managed to relax almost too well. With my head pillowed on the ledgers and my back resting on the boards, I'd finally gotten to that druglike state between waking and sleeping where your thoughts and your unconscious mind become almost indistinguishable and it's hard to say whether you're asleep or awake.

I was awake enough to hear the steps on the porch outside, at any rate, and by the time the two men got inside I was fully alert. I couldn't make out any features, of course, but in the moment that they were briefly silhouetted in the doorway I could see that they were certainly bulky enough to be two of the three I'd met already.

In my drifting state of a few minutes before, I'd almost thought I was making some sense of the whole confused caper, but the sight of the two gorillas brought me to a hard reality that had to be dealt with on a purely physical level. They weren't something I could drift and dream about any longer.

They stood for several minutes, almost motionless, probably waiting until they could see a little better. I could make them out only as darker blobs in the general darkness, and I was hoping they might have brought a flashlight. Not that I wanted them to turn it on and examine their surroundings too closely. I was fairly certain they wouldn't see me, but I didn't want them even to try.

They were very quiet, and I found myself practically holding my breath. If it had been quiet earlier, it was deadly still now. I hadn't heard a car pass for so long that I couldn't even remember when the last one had been.

After what must have been about ten minutes, though it seemed much longer, they began moving around the warehouse, still without speaking a word. No light was turned on, but they moved confidently, as if they knew where they were and could see well enough.

One of them searched the room below me, which had the only window in the place. The door creaked when he opened it. I suppose the window gave him enough light to inspect the place. It was too small to require a lengthy investigation.

The other man moved to the opposite end of the warehouse, then returned along the other side. They met in the middle.

"So now what?" one of them said. His voice was so loud in the silence that I almost jumped. "We wait for a couple of hours?"

"That's right," the other said. "We screw up this time, Hobbes gonna have our asses."

I assumed that Hobbes was the absent third man. I still wasn't sure which one he was, but something about these two—at least as well as I could see them—indicated that neither of them was the man I'd fought with. Something about the way they moved, the way they bulked in the darkness. I wasn't sure. But I thought that Hobbes was probably that one. And he was missing.

"Anything to sit on in this dump?" the first man said.

"You can go in there and sit on the john."

"Funny." The first man went over to the scale and sat on the platform. I could hear it clank. It wasn't much better than sitting on the floor.

"You bring your gun?" the second man said. He sounded like he was from deep East Texas.

"Damn right." The first man shifted on the scale to bring out a pistol. As he moved he rocked the balance arm, and the weights that were sitting on it clattered to the floor. In the confined space they sounded like an accident in an industrial foundry.

"Goddamn, goddamn!" the second man yelled. "What the fuck was that?"

"Just something on this goddamn scale," the first man said. His voice was a little shaky. "Calm down."

"Goddamn, I almost shot you! You gotta keep quiet!"

"Fuck it, Kirk, get hold of yourself. You're worse'n an old woman."

"I can't help it. I don't mind beatin' a half-crippled guy up, but this killin' business gets me nervous."

The first man stood up. "Me too. But we can't fuck up again. I'd rather be a little nervous than get Hobbes pissed off."

"I guess so." Kirk didn't sound too sure, even about that.

I was wondering how to resolve the situation. Obviously they were there to try killing Dino again, not to give him Sharon. The Mauser was lying beside me. A TV private eye would just yell something like "Freeze, you scumbags!" and then blow the guys away. I'd never done anything like that. Besides, as tense as Kirk and his buddy were, they might blow *me* away before I could get the second word out of my mouth.

On the other hand, they were so nervous that they might just shoot each other. I reached as quietly as I could into one of the boxes and put my hand around a roll of adding machine tape, intending to throw it to the other end of the warehouse. Then when their backs were turned, I could yell "Freeze!"

It was a good idea, and it might even have worked. I just didn't get a chance to try it. When I shifted position to throw the tape, I brushed my hip against the sack I'd brought with me. The two Big Red bottles clinked together.

It wasn't much of a sound, really, but it seemed as loud as a six-car pileup to me. It must have sounded like considerably more to Kirk and his pal.

Almost instantly a light was turned on. They'd had one, after all, probably the better to spotlight Dino with when it came time to shoot him.

I flattened out behind the boxes. They didn't know where, exactly, the noise had come from. They swept the light around the entire warehouse, and I thought they might miss me. Then the light came to rest on the boxes in front of me. Two thin beams seeped between narrow spaces between the cardboard sides.

The light moved on, then returned. No one was saying a word. If they fired at the boxes, I was fairly well protected by the rolls of paper and the ledgers, but it wasn't a place I'd like to stay for an extended length of time.

The light held steady. I didn't move. I hardly breathed. I began to sweat, not so much with fear as with uncertainty.

Still no one spoke, but I heard footsteps. I picked up the Mauser. If they fired through the boards beneath me, I was a dead man. I hadn't been as smart as I'd thought when I chose my hiding place.

But one of them wasn't so smart, either. After all, he was the one holding the light.

I rolled to one side, brought up the Mauser, and snapped off a shot at the light. There wasn't time to do any aiming.

There was a dull splat, a groan, and the light was flying

through the air. It hit the floor and rolled, pointing away from the rest room. It was almost as dark as it had been before.

"Jerry, Jerry!" the man who must have been Kirk said in a hoarse whisper.

Jerry groaned. I had no idea where I'd hit him, but he obviously wasn't feeling too good about it.

It was quiet for about two seconds. Then Kirk fired his pistol. I could see a flash of light, almost as if a faulty flashbulb had gone off. The bullet thudded into one of the boxes. Dust flew.

Then Kirk was moving, toward the rest room. I gave him just enough time to get there, then swung over the side, holding the edge with one hand. It wasn't much of a drop, a few inches maybe. I let go and landed without hurting the knee.

Kirk was inside, I was outside. I knew where he was, but I didn't think I'd made enough noise to let him know where I was.

I was wrong. Suddenly he stepped round the side of the bathroom and fired twice.

Fortunately, he didn't know exactly where I was, and the bullets zipped by me and thwanged into the tin wall.

I fired back and Kirk gave a strangled cry, tossing his pistol away. He crashed to the floor. He didn't move again.

Jerry wasn't moving, either. I walked to the flashlight and picked it up, then directed the yellow beam toward first Jerry, then Kirk.

Long shadows extended from the bodies. It was an eerie sight. Jerry appeared to be breathing. Kirk didn't.

I walked over to Kirk. I'd shot him right in the nose. He'd fallen on his side. I didn't look at the back of his head too closely. A sour sweetness rose in my throat. I swallowed it.

Jerry wasn't much better off than Kirk, and there was a lot more blood, most of it on the front of his shirt where he was holding his hands. He was alive, but only just. I didn't want to lift his shirt to see what was under it.

He looked at me and tried to say something, but only blood came out of his mouth.

I walked to the rest room and vomited in the toilet.

When I came back out, Jerry was dead.

They had come here to kill Dino, and either one of them would have killed me. Looking at them, I knew they were two of the three who'd beaten me at The Sidepocket.

But I hadn't wanted to kill them. I hadn't intended it.

I was still holding the Mauser. I stuck it in my waistband. Then I turned the light on my hand. I guess I expected it to be covered in blood. I started shaking and had to go sit on the scale.

After a while I was all right. I climbed back up on the ceiling of the restroom and got the sack. Then I got out of there.

I went back to Evelyn's. There was a light on, and I knocked on the door.

"My God," Evelyn said when she saw me. I didn't ask why.

"Where's Dino?" I asked.

"In the bedroom." She was looking at me the way you look at someone who's walked away from a plane crash. I walked by her and to the bedroom.

"What happened to you?" Dino said. He was sitting up in the bed. "You look like hell."

I told him what had happened.

"You didn't call the cops?"

"Evelyn can call them," I said. "Anonymously. She can say she heard gunshots." I looked over my shoulder at Evelyn, who had followed me to the room. "Can you do that?"

She nodded and went out.

"They would have got me this time," Dino said. "I really think they would have got me this time."

"Maybe not," I said.

I was beginning to calm down. My hands had been shaking on the wheel of the car all the way to the house, but they were almost steady now. I wished it were all over, but it wasn't. Not quite.

"I just can't figure it," Dino said. "Who'd want to kill me?"

"I think I know," I said. I'd known since I calmed down from the shooting and thought about something I'd heard in the warehouse. "I think we'll be hearing from him in a little while, probably around three o'clock or so."

"You know? Tell me, by God." Dino sat up straighter, wincing slightly from the effort. "What do you mean, we'll be hearing?"

"If I were sure, I'd tell you. But there's still a chance that I'm wrong. Let's just wait. It can't take much longer than that."

I looked at my watch. It wasn't even one o'clock. The whole scene at the warehouse had taken only a few minutes, never mind that it had seemed like a lifetime. Or two.

"Look," Dino said. "You gotta tell me."

"Not yet. I'm going in and lie down on the couch. If we don't get a call in a couple of hours, then I'll tell you what I think. I hope I'm wrong."

Evelyn walked in. "I called the police. They started asking me questions. I hung up."

"Good," I said.

The call would be recorded, but I doubted that it could ever be traced. Too short. I left them alone in the bedroom and went to lie down.

The ring of the telephone woke me up. I was surprised that I'd been asleep, but I've been told that sleep is a common reaction to stress. Evelyn answered the phone.

"Hello," she said. Then she did a lot of listening.

The two men hadn't gone back to wherever they'd come from. Anyone who'd gone near the warehouse to see what had happened to them would have encountered the cops, but I didn't think the caller had been there. The failure of Jerry and Kirk to return would have spoken for itself.

"Ask to speak to Sharon," I said.

Evelyn looked at me, nodded. "I want to talk to Sharon." She listened. "I don't believe you. I want to talk to her." There was another pause. I could tell when Sharon started talking. Evelyn's face changed. Then she was crying.

I got up and took the phone from her hand. There was no one on the other end.

"They hung up," Evelyn said, wiping the back of her hand across her eyes. "You knew, didn't you. Dino said you knew."

"I thought I did. I didn't want to be right, but I was afraid I was. I should have known from the first."

It took the remark about beating up a crippled guy to clue me in, finally. Who but Ray or Dino could have told them that? And it wasn't Dino. I should have known when they went for my knee, but I thought they'd gotten lucky.

Dino was yelling from the bedroom. When we didn't answer, he walked in. I don't know how I had looked to him earlier, but I was sure he looked worse than I had. It was hurting him to walk.

"What happened, goddamnit? Talk to me, Tru. Who was it?"

"It was Ray," Evelyn said.

Dino looked as if someone had hit him in the gut with a Louisville Slugger. He shuffled over to a chair and sat down like an old man.

"Ray?" he said.

"Ray," I said. "How many people knew Sharon was your

daughter? Maybe quite a few, according to Sally West, but how many of them cared? How many of them even remembered that they knew it? It didn't matter to anyone. Except to Ray." *Yas, suh. Ah jus' brangs the dranks.*

Dino shook his head. "I don't get it."

"Ray was always second class," I said. "Your uncles took him in, and then you, but what did it ever get him? He almost made it out, almost made it to the pros, but he didn't. So he came back here. To what? To watch you watching television. To get the drinks when you called him. To go fetch somebody you needed to talk to."

Dino was still not getting it. "But . . . I gave him money. He had a place to live. Goddammit, he was my friend!"

"It wasn't enough," I said. "You remember what this island used to be. You remember the uncles. I guess Ray did, too. He must have thought you'd be like them. High living. Top of the line."

"That just . . . wasn't my style."

"I guess he found that out. You're like the Island, Dino. You're not aging gracefully."

He looked up at me. "You're no fucking prize yourself, Tru."

"Hell, I know that. I've been hiding as much as you."

"You're sure about Ray?"

"I am," Evelyn said. "It was him."

"Those guys at The Sidepocket went for my knee," I said. "Who told them to do that? The clincher is the one I should have clicked on earlier, though. They knew about Evelyn, but how could they be sure you were here? Why not call your house? But Ray would have known you were here. I went by to see him earlier today—yesterday. He wasn't worried about you at all. No wonder. He knew you'd gotten away from the men at the airport, and he knew who you were with. Everything came up Ray, but I just didn't see it. I didn't want to see it, I guess."

"Hell," Dino said. "How could you? You weren't looking in the right direction."

"I'm sure he went to Ferguson when he found out that Sharon and Terry Shelton hung out at The Sidepocket and that Ferguson rounded up the strong arm boys. I don't know who killed Shelton and Ferguson, but it had to be Ray or one of the others. He's eliminating everyone who was in on it."

"But why?" Evelyn said.

"I'm not sure even Ray knows. I just think he doesn't want any witnesses around."

"Between you and him, there won't be many," Dino said.

"Thanks," I told him. "I needed that. But I don't think he was counting on me to do his job for him tonight."

"What about Sharon?" Dino said.

"I think he's kept her alive this long just in case. Just in case something went wrong. He's been good at covering his bets. He had the guy watching the Shelton house in case I showed up there. Now he's got something that you want, which means that you'll be pretty sure to do what he tells you."

"I still can't believe it," Dino said. "Ray."

"Ray," I said. "Good old Ray."

"So," Dino said. "Where does all this leave us?"

I looked at Evelyn.

"He sounded strange, very upset," she said. "At first I couldn't make out what he was saying. He was . . . sort of choked up, or . . . I don't really know." She shook her head. "Anyway, he wants us—all of us—to meet him somewhere. He didn't say where. He just said, 'Tell Dino. He knows.' "

"Do you?" I said.

Dino looked puzzled. "You said he sounded weird, Evelyn, but this is really weird. How should I know where he wants us to meet him?"

"I don't know," she said. "But that's what he said. 'Tell Dino.' "

"Think about it," I said. "It can't be far, or he wouldn't

be able to get there easily. He had those tough guys stashed practically in your front yard."

"I just can't figure it," Dino said. "You think he's at the house?"

"No," I said. "He's had Sharon somewhere right here on the Island all along, and she isn't at your house."

"Well, I have another house—"

"Where?"

"It's a place I bought a few years ago, when I was thinking of moving out of town. But I couldn't do it, not after I thought about it. Too much beach and water."

Just like a native, I thought. Wouldn't want to live in sight of the Gulf. "Where?" I said again.

"Down past the west beach."

"Many other houses around?"

"I haven't been there in at least a year. I was thinking about putting it on the market. But no, there weren't many houses around last time I saw it."

That didn't necessarily mean there weren't any by now, but there was a good chance that Ray might have seen the place as a good hideaway.

"Ray know about this place?"

"Yeah. He was with me the whole time I was looking."

"That's our best bet then." I turned to Evelyn. "Did he give any instructions?"

"Yes. We're all to arrive in one car. Yours. He says he'd know it anywhere."

"That's it?"

"Yes."

"What about Sharon?"

"She sounded scared. Really scared."

"She has a right to be," I said. "So am I."

▽

1 7

THE GULF BREEZE NEVER really stops blowing. It hit us in the face as we stepped out the front door, cool and damp in the early February morning. The sky was clouded over almost entirely, but that could change at any minute. As it was, we were going to be operating mainly in the darkness.

Evelyn got in the backseat of the Subaru. She was so small that she could almost be comfortable. Dino sat in the bucket seat opposite me.

I was carrying extra bullets for the Mauser in the pocket of my jeans, and before I started the car I reloaded the clip.

"You steal that gun off a dead Nazi?" Dino said.

I didn't answer. If he was trying to be funny, he wasn't making it. I stuck the pistol back in the back waistband of my jeans. It would rub my back as I drove, but I didn't want to chance trying to get to it if I put it under the seat.

We drove down Seawall Boulevard, past the pier where Dino's uncles once had had their biggest casino; past the huge Flagship hotel, also built on a pier, which had showered huge panes of glass during Hurricane Alicia; through the old Fort Crockett area, where Dino had once gotten a speeding ticket when we were teenagers; past the San Luis Hotel and the Holiday Inn. The Gulf was only a few yards to our left, but none of us noticed it.

Then we slipped down off the seawall, down to the level of the old Island itself. The area behind the seawall was not actually at sea level. After the famous 1900 storm, the level of the entire city had been raised. Sand was dredged out of the channel and distributed all over the Island. Those houses already on stilts just had sand stashed under them; others were actually jacked up until the job was done. For months, people got around the town on rickety elevated walkways. It was quite an engineering feat, not to mention an inconvenience, but everyone thought it would be worth the trouble if it would guarantee that the Island would never be completely underwater again.

Because it lacked the protection of a seawall and was exactly at sea level, the west end of the Island had been slow to develop. In fact, only in recent years had there been a building boom of any sort there. Now, if you drove to Jamaica Beach, or Indian Beach, or Karankawa Beach, or Sea Isle, or any of the other little areas scattered down the length of the Island, you could see hundreds of quiet expensive beach houses, all of them built on stilts ten or twelve feet or more off the ground. The Island is very narrow there, and in any of the houses you happen to choose you can see the Gulf from one side and the West Bay from the other. Unless, of course, another house is in the way.

Almost as soon as we dropped down to sea level, the name of the road changed from Seawall Boulevard to Termini Road. I didn't like it. It sounded too much like *terminal* to suit me.

I turned on the radio, but I couldn't pick up an AM station. I listened to the static for a minute and turned it off.

"Remember when we used to drive around the Island when we were kids?" Dino said. "We'd listen to that station that had its studios in Ft. Worth and its transmitter in Coahuila, Mexico."

"XEG," I said.

Dino smiled at the memory. "That's the one. Remember those guys we used to listen to? Don and Earl, your Christian gospel singers? Brother J. Charles Jessup?"

I remembered. "Who was it that had the magic picture of Jesus Christ? The one where you stared at the picture and then looked up at the sky. The picture was supposed to appear in the sky."

"I don't know," Dino said. "Don and Earl, maybe?"

"You two are kidding me," Evelyn said from the backseat.

"Not us," I said. "You don't think Jimmy Swaggart and Jim Bakker just *happened*, do you?"

"I guess I never gave it much thought one way or the other," she said.

On our left now as we drove was mostly undeveloped land, flat and featureless in the darkness. It wasn't much different in the daylight. The sand was covered with a few low-growing plants, but that was all. The big-money developing was down on the beach.

"We used to think they'd sneak over the border after sundown and crank that transmitter up to about a million watts," Dino said. "You could pick up that station anywhere in the world."

"Magic pictures of Jesus just for sending a little donation," I said. "I wonder what the Laplanders thought about that?"

Dino didn't answer. "We're coming up on Ten Mile Road," he said. "Turn right and get on Stewart Road there."

Stewart parallels Termini, more or less, but it's a lot different. Any houses on Termini are likely to be new, expensive, and well-cared for. A lot of the houses on Stewart, and there aren't many, are likely to be the opposite.

"Your house is on Stewart Road?" I said.

"That's right." He shrugged. I didn't know whether the shrug was an apology or whether his bandage was itching.

At Ten Mile Road I turned right. Almost at once I turned left again, this time on Stewart. Now the land on both the left and right was undeveloped. Every now and then we passed a dilapidated corral, and I could see the dark shapes of cattle lying in the scrubby grass.

"You'd better stop here," Dino said.

There weren't any houses nearby, but about a quarter of a mile down the road there was one that looked like a geodesic dome on stilts. If it had started walking toward us, it would have looked like one of the Martian machines in the old *War of the Worlds*.

"Is that it?" I asked, pointing.

"No," Dino said. "It's the one a little farther along."

I looked but I didn't see anything that looked like a beach house. "Where?"

Dino pointed with his good arm. I still didn't see anything except what I took to be a large clump of brush. "I'm not sure I know which one you're talking about," I said.

"Look," Dino said. "I hate those things sticking up twelve feet into the air. I'd get a nosebleed just climbing up to the living room. I bought an old ranch house."

"I guess you can't see the water from it, either."

"You can't see a damn thing from it. It's like covered up with bushes and stuff. It's an old house, and it's been flooded a time or two, but it was something I thought I might be able to live in. But when it came right down to it, I couldn't leave town."

"So that's where Ray is."

"Got to be, if he said I'd know where he was. There's no place else except the whorehouse, and that's long gone."

"OK. So why are we stopped?"

"I thought you might not want to go in cold. You might want to know a little about the layout."

Dino was thinking better than I was, but then I never claimed to be an assault tactician. "You're right," I said.

"I'm getting nervous," Evelyn said. "Is it all right if I smoke?"

I didn't like people to smoke in my car. You could never get the odor out. But if Ray had his way tonight, it probably wouldn't make a hell of a lot of difference to me anyway. "Go ahead," I said. "Open the window, though." No use in giving up entirely.

There was a brief flare in the back as Evelyn flicked a lighter; then I could smell the cigarette burning. She opened the window of the bay side and the smoke drifted out.

"So what's the house like?" I said.

"You see the roof?" Dino said.

I stared at the clump of trees and bushes and thought I could make out a roofline, though I wasn't certain. "I think so."

"OK. Well, the front of the house is more or less facing us. There's an oyster-shell road leading to the front, but it doesn't stop at the door. It goes on by, down to a little turnaround. No garage. Those bushes cover most of the house, even most of the windows. That's why I liked it, I guess."

Even more of a womb than where he was living now. I was surprised he hadn't moved in.

"There's an opening for the front, though," he said. "It's not on stilts, but the house is up three or so feet off the ground. There's a front porch, concrete, with banisters, and there's steps leading up to it. The steps are all clear of brush and about six feet wide. Then there's the front door, right on the porch."

I looked toward the house. If there were lights on, I couldn't see them. It was about as isolated as you could get on the Island. "How far from the porch to the road?"

Dino thought about it. "I haven't been out here much

lately. I guess about fifty feet. There's a sidewalk up to the porch."

Fifty feet. I was accurate with a pistol, and tonight I had been lucky. If killing two men was lucky. But fifty feet was quite a distance for accuracy with a handgun. To hit any of us at that range, Ray would have to be very good, and at sixty feet he'd have to be better than that. Of course if Dino had underestimated the distance, or if Ray had a rifle, or . . . a hundred or so other things.

I looked at the dark shape of the house and bushes again. Somewhere in there was Ray, nursing a grudge created by his own imagining but one that had been building for years. His mind wasn't working normally, and he had Sharon Matthews as a hostage. I hated to start the car and drive down there.

Evelyn tossed her cigarette out the back window. "I'm ready whenever you are," she said.

I started the car.

"How do we play it?" Dino said.

"By ear," I told him.

We turned right onto the shell road and drove very slowly toward the house, which sat well off the road, at least a couple of hundred yards. I still couldn't see any lights.

When we got near the house, I slowed even more, taking us down to about five miles an hour. I wasn't stalling, but I wasn't in any hurry, either.

"I'm going to stop in front," I said, having just made the decision. "That puts me next to the house, and I'm the one with the gun. Besides, you're the one he wants. That way you'll have me between you and him."

Dino grunted, which I took to mean that he thought it was a good plan. Or a rotten one. The tires crunched on the shell road, and the dark bulk of the house grew in front of us as we approached. The clouds were breaking up a little now, but there was hardly any moonlight. The darkness was nearly complete.

The road curved slightly to take us in front of the house, and as we rounded the curve the porch light snapped on. It was only a small bulb, maybe a sixty watt, but it looked like the sun.

I assumed that the light was my cue to stop the car, so I did, keeping an eye on the porch. There was a black screen door, which was suddenly pushed open.

Ray came through the door. There was a girl with him. It looked like a scene from a bad movie. Ray had his arm around the girl's throat in a choke hold. In his right hand he held a revolver that he kept pointed toward the girl's head.

"My God. It's Sharon," Evelyn said.

Dino didn't say anything, and I didn't look at him. I was looking at Ray.

Ray didn't look so good. His eyes were wild, and he looked as if he might be sweating despite the breeze that whipped the bushes and jerked their shadows around.

Sharon looked worse, hardly like the girl in the photo Dino had given me. Her face was drawn and her hair was lank and greasy. She hadn't been giving much attention to her appearance in the past few days. She looked scared. I didn't blame her.

I turned off the car's engine and rolled down my window. "Why don't you let her go, Ray?" I said.

Ray laughed; then his mouth twisted and cut the laugh off. "You been causing me trouble, Tru," he said. "I thought you'd caved in, but you didn't cave far enough."

I'd caved too far, I thought. I'd missed things all around that I should have seen. At first I was too involved in my own misery, and then when I finally began to come out of it, to respond to someone else's trouble for a change, I was still too screwed up to get everything straight in my mind.

I didn't say any of that to Ray, however. I said, "You can

have the money. We brought it for you. Just let the girl go."

Ray acted as if I hadn't spoken. "Get out of the car," he said. "All of you. You try anything, and there'll be little pieces of this girl's head all over this porch."

"Me first," I told Dino. "Then you. Then Evelyn. Keep the car between you and him." I got out.

"Turn around and put your hands on the car roof," Ray said.

I did what he said. Dino got out on the other side. He moved a little forward, and Evelyn followed him.

"Now what?" I said.

"Now we see where you've got your gun," Ray said. "I know what happened at the warehouse. Hobbes."

I heard someone step out of the bushes behind me. Ray had been covered all along. Something hard pressed into my back just above the Mauser and Hobbes ran his hand down my legs, inseam and outseam, then up to the front of my stomach.

"He's clean," Hobbes said.

I sneaked a look at him. He was the one who'd hit my knee, the one I'd fought with at Shelton's. He was good with his hands, but he wasn't much at a body search.

I started to turn around.

"Don't!" Ray said. There was a sharp cry from the girl, as if he had tightened his grip on her throat or mashed the gun barrel into her temple.

"I don't understand, Ray," Dino said.

"Sure you don't," Ray said. "You step around in front of the car. Very slowly."

Dino moved to the front of the Subaru. I was calculating distances. We weren't fifty feet from the porch as I had hoped, but we were about forty. The light hardly reached us. There was a chance that Ray wouldn't hit us, but Hobbes would. And Ray could certainly kill Sharon.

"Let me tell you something, Dino," Ray said. "You *owe* me, Dino."

"Owe?" Dino said. "I—"

"*Owe!*" Ray's voice would have carried a mile if it hadn't been whipped away by the wind. "Owe," he repeated, more calmly this time.

"You were always the ones, you and Tru. You let me tag along, but I was just the tame nigger. I was just as good a football player as either one of you, but you were the ones who got your pictures in the paper. You were the ones who got to go to the good schools. You were the ones—"

"Wait a minute," Dino said, putting up a hand. "You got to go to school. You even got a tryout with the pros."

"Check that fucker out, Hobbes," Ray said. "Maybe he's the one with the gun. Put your hands on the car, Dino."

Dino put his hands on the hood. Hobbes gave him the same treatment he'd given me. "Clean," he said.

"Dumb as dirt," Ray said. "But I was the one who had to go to that nigger school."

"Look, Ray, you were good, good enough for the pros," Dino said. "You could've been a big star—"

"—if it wasn't for the accident," Ray finished. "And what about that accident, Dino?"

Dino didn't say anything.

"I believe you said 'Let's celebrate, Ray. You and Tommy and me.' That's right, isn't it Dino? And you had Tommy drive by a 7-Eleven so you could buy us some beers, and Tommy never could hold his liquor. Isn't that about right, Dino?"

"Yeah," Dino said. "I guess that's about right."

So Dino had been in the car that night, too. I hadn't known about that part of it, had never asked. Dino had ended two football careers, Ray's and mine, inadvertently but effectively. Well, it happens.

Right then, I didn't care. I was more interested in watching Hobbes, who was now in front of the hood of the car and to my left. Only Ray was behind me, but he still had the girl.

". . . so I've been fetching ever since." Ray was talking again, and even though I missed some of it, I got the gist. He really knew how to hold a grudge.

I sneaked a look over my shoulder. Ray didn't seem to mind, so I dropped my arms and started to turn around.

Hobbes saw the movement, though he was watching Dino, and started to swing his pistol in my direction.

"It's all right," Ray said. "Let him get comfortable. He needs to hear this, too."

I leaned back against the car and folded my arms across my chest. "Why me?" I said.

"You were the fair-haired boy," Ray said. "You got all the glory that Dino didn't. Everybody was so busy writing about you in the sports pages that there wasn't any space for the nigger. I should have been at Southern Cal, man, or USC."

"So where does the girl fit in?" Sharon looked even worse than she had earlier. Ray practically had the gun stuck in her ear, and the hold he had on her must have been practically crushing her windpipe.

Ray laughed. "The girl?" he said. "I thought you'd figured that out by now, Tru. Hell, this was all her idea."

$\triangledown$

1 8

S HARON STRUGGLED AGAINST RAY'S arm and appeared to be trying to speak, but Ray just clamped a little tighter on her throat and stuck the revolver barrel a little farther into her ear.

Well, it was nice to know that I'd been right about one thing at least. "You told her, didn't you, Ray? About Dino."

"I told her."

"So the kidnapping was all her idea, resentment against the father she'd never known."

"You got it."

"You're a liar, Ray." I thought he might be bothered by the accusation, but it went right by him. "You planted the idea. She might have thought it was hers, but it was yours."

He was unconcerned. "Maybe."

"So why did you kill Shelton and Ferguson?"

"Who says I killed them?"

I was watching Hobbes out of the corner of my eye. "You don't mean you're going to try to lay the murders off on someone else?"

Hobbes wasn't bothered by my remark in the least.

"We've discussed that," Ray said. "We're going to blame them on you."

"Oh," I said.

"I was hoping you'd bring your pistol, but that's all right. We'll find it anyway. You can use this one." He wiggled his pistol. Sharon winced.

"What for?" I said.

"The big shoot-out. The one where Dino and I come to deliver the ransom money and everyone gets killed. Everyone but me, that is. And Hobbes, of course."

"I wouldn't be too sure of that if I were you, Hobbes," I said. "He didn't mind killing Ferguson and Shelton."

"There you go again," Ray said. I wondered if he was a fan of Ronald Reagan. "Who says I killed them? As a matter of fact, it was Hobbes who did those little jobs. He understands the necessity for having as few loose ends as possible."

I could hardly believe this was the Ray I'd known for so long. Of course I had no way of measuring his bitterness, which seemed to be much stronger than I had first thought. I wondered what I would have finally become if I had let my own injury fester in my mind as much as Ray had allowed his to do.

"Is that all they were, loose ends?" I said.

"Shelton was getting antsy. I should never have let him out of my sight in the first place. He would have cracked. Ferguson was greedy. Neither one was helping me any."

I figured that as long as I could keep him talking we were still alive, so I was going to ask him about how he got involved with Ferguson when I noticed that I couldn't see Evelyn any longer. She was so short that her head was barely higher than the car roof anyway. I didn't know where she was, but better that one of us should get away than none. Hobbes was watching Dino, and Ray was watching me. In the darkness, no one had been watching Evelyn.

"And you're going to kill the girl, too."

"Absolutely," Ray said. He was quite happy. "Dino gets to watch. That's the good part. And there's no time like the present." He shoved Sharon in front of him, and she fell from the porch to the sidewalk, catching herself with her hands. Ray took a two-handed grip on his pistol and pointed it at her.

Evelyn hadn't left after all. She came charging from behind the car, screaming. "No!" she said. "No!"

Ray twisted and fired at her.

I dropped into a crouch and pulled out the Parabellum. This was war, all right. A bullet smashed into the door of the Subaru behind me.

I shot at Ray. The slug chipped off a piece of the porch banister and smacked into the wall.

Dino must have jumped Hobbes. I could hear them struggling in the shell road.

Ray fired again. Flame leaped from the end of his pistol muzzle. The bullet hit the drive in front of me and gouged up pieces of shell and a cloud of dust. Something stung my cheek.

Evelyn had managed to reach Sharon where she lay on the walk. Ray fired at them. One of them yelled in pain. Then Ray was off and running.

I wanted to help Dino with Hobbes. I wanted to do something for Sharon and Evelyn.

But most of all, I wanted Ray. I went after him.

Dino and Hobbes were grunting and groaning on the ground. Dino was louder. I didn't know what had happened to Hobbes's gun. I just hoped that Dino could handle him and that his wound wouldn't be too great a handicap. Dino had been a bull once; maybe he still was.

Ray had taken off down the road. I followed it to the turnaround and saw that he was headed for the bay. I wondered if he had a boat tied up out there.

My knee was all right for the few yards to the end of the road, but things got markedly worse when I got off the relatively smooth surface. The weeds were thick and pulled at my ankles, but the sand was worse. Much worse.

Even running on a flat, even road takes its toll. The toll is more or less, depending on the biomechanics of your body, the way your feet hit, the way your bones twist. Sand makes everything worse. Your feet sink in, and the twisting is all magnified. The fact that there are mounds and holes adds to the misery. After twenty yards, my knee was screaming. Ray was gaining easily.

Then he stopped. He turned, braced his right arm with his left hand, and fired at me.

He didn't come close. He was at least thirty yards away, a long way for a pistol shot under the best conditions, and he had been running. Try running a hundred yards and then firing a pistol someday. You'd be lucky to hit a wall thirty yards away. Besides, it was dark. The wind was chasing black and gray shadows across the sky, and every now and then a thin moon showed through, but certainly not enough to shoot by. It's surprising how well your eyes adapt to the darkness after a while, but few men have the night vision of cats.

In other words, I didn't feel too threatened by Ray's firing at me. I just kept on running.

Ray saw that I was gaining. He lowered his pistol and ran.

I got almost to where he'd been standing when I felt a familiar and terrible feeling, but it was too late to stop. It was as if my left leg were going up a stairway while my right leg was going down. The knee had given way.

I put my hands out to break the fall and felt my palms slide on the sand, scraping the skin. I'd dropped the pistol.

My face hit the sand right after my hands. I'd turned it to the right, so only the left side got the skin rubbed off.

I looked to see where Ray was. He'd realized I wasn't behind him anymore, and he was looking around to see where I'd gone. He was silhouetted against the dark sky and would have made a good target if I'd been a little closer. And if I'd had the pistol. I felt around with my hand to find it. I brushed through the weeds and sand, and then I felt the metal of the pistol barrel. I pulled it to me and tried to brush some of the sand off against my sweatshirt.

Ray had started back toward me. I lay still and pointed the Mauser at him, trying to breathe slowly and steadily, bracing my arm on the ground and gripping my wrist with the opposite hand. I would be pretty hard for him to see, since I was wearing dark clothing. Maybe I could wait until he got close enough.

He saw me too soon. He stopped and fired, but the bullet was well to my left. I took a deep breath, let it out slowly, and squeezed the trigger.

Ray yelled and spun around. I'd hit him somewhere, maybe in the arm. He was running again.

I tried to get to my feet and finally made it. There was no question of my running, though. What I did was hobble, my right leg dragging almost uselessly along.

Ray got down to the edge of the water. He stopped, pressing his left arm tightly to his side, fumbling in his pocket with his right hand. The pistol must have been in his left, but I didn't see it. He was reloading the cylinder.

It didn't take him long, and then he was moving along parallel to the water. He was going slower now, but he was still getting farther and farther ahead of me. He kept looking to his right for something. I thought again about a boat.

There wasn't any boat. The next thing I knew, Ray was out into the water, headed deeper.

I remembered what a boating friend of mine had told me once. "Sailing in the bay is OK," he said. "But you've got to watch out. It's really shallow. Why you could walk across it if you tried." He laughed. "Not really, but if you knew where to go and when to swim a little, you could make it without too much trouble."

Ray must have figured it was worth a try. By the way he had been looking, I thought he must have had a marker, some light on the opposite shore, to tell him when to hit the water.

He was sloshing through it now, up to his waist. The good thing was that it slowed him down.

I got to the edge and looked out at Ray. He didn't look back. I stepped into the water.

It was cold. I was in only up over my ankles, and the chill went right through to the bone. I went on out. If Ray could do it, I could.

The water worked to my advantage as it got deeper. It took some of the weight off my leg, and I was able to move as fast as Ray. Of course, I was so cold that my teeth were chattering. I was shaking too much to hit an elephant with a pistol shot, much less a man. I kept on, trying as best I could to follow Ray's path.

I was getting nearer, almost within range. Then Ray disappeared, just sank right under.

I stopped. It was dark, and maybe he lost his way. I stood, waiting for him to surface, the wind tugging at me and almost freezing my sweatshirt to my body.

Suddenly Ray popped out of the water, showering drops all around.

He scared the hell out of me. He was so close that I could see him clearly. He'd been swimming toward me under the water. He was smarter than I was, that was for sure.

He was firing the pistol wildly, however. Blue flames spurted from the barrel.

I sank under the water. Never let it be said that I'm a slow learner. The scrapes on my hands and face sizzled when the saltwater hit them.

I have no idea how long I was under. I wasn't used to holding my breath, so it probably wasn't long. I stayed down until my lungs were burning. I thought about Ray, wondering if he thought he'd hit me. I knew he was reloading, waiting for me to come up.

I eased a little way to my left, gripped the pistol, and popped up. I held the pistol down to make sure the water drained out of the barrel. The wind hit me like a bucket of shaved ice.

Ray was nowhere in sight.

I looked all around, hoping to be able to see bubbles on the surface of the water if he was releasing his breath.

I didn't see anything except the slight chop on the water caused by the wind.

There was a huge splash behind me. I started turning. It was as if things were happening in slow motion. I got half turned before the shooting started.

Over the sound of the pistol, I could hear Ray's screaming. He wasn't screaming out words. It was just noise. Rage, I suppose, or maybe the saltwater was just hurting his wound. Or it could be that he'd gone completely around the bend.

I went under again.

In a way, Ray had the advantage of me. He knew about how long I could stay under, so he could wait to go down himself. My only chance was to outmaneuver him. I tried to decide whether to try getting so far away that he couldn't possibly hit me or simply to head for the shore. Either way, he might outguess me. I opted for the shore.

The water was cold, but at least it seemed warmer underneath it than in the wind above. I held my breath as long as I could. I was just about to surface when I collided with something.

It was Ray.

I tried to move away to get to the air, but he was on me too quickly, flailing at me, trying to get a grip on me so he could hold me under.

Somehow he got his left hand tangled in my hair. He started trying to hit me with the pistol, but he couldn't do much damage under the water. Then he tried raking my face with the barrel. I felt the tip of the sight rip the skin of my jaw.

I was more worried about getting a breath than about what he could do to me with the pistol. I struggled for the surface, but he clubbed me on the temple. There wasn't much force in the blow, but there was enough to keep me down.

I fought back by jabbing him in the stomach with the Mauser. I shoved as hard as I could, concentrating all my force on the small spot of the attack. It was so dark under the water that I couldn't see a thing, so I had no real idea of exactly where I was hitting him. I wasn't going to last much longer. I would have pulled the trigger, but I was afraid to. I didn't know what might happen. The barrel was full of water. There was water outside, too, and maybe the forces would balance out, but I didn't want to take the chance of having the pistol blow up in my hand.

Ray loosened his grip on my hair as I jabbed him for the third time. I flipped over and kicked backward as hard as I could, then shot out of the water like an undersea missile. I was gasping, burning lungfuls of air, and trying to get my footing, hold on to the pistol, and spot Ray.

It took me a second or two to realize that I wasn't going to be able to get my footing because there wasn't any footing. We'd drifted over a hole. I tried to tread water and calm down.

Ray was easing to the side about twenty feet in front of me. I could barely see his head atop the dark water. I moved in the same direction.

He got his footing first, and his shoulders rose out of the chop. He fired twice. Both bullets thunked into the water to my left, sounding almost as if they were hitting Sheetrock.

I was exhausted. My knee was throbbing and I could almost feel it swelling. My scraped skin was frying on both my face and hands. The cut on my jaw felt as if it had electricity running through it. But I still didn't want to have to shoot Ray.

He'd tried to kill Dino once and tried to set him up a

second time when the first attempt failed. He'd certainly had both Shelton and Ferguson killed, though he hadn't done it himself. He'd abused Sharon Matthews, even if he was telling the truth about the kidnapping being her idea. He may have killed either her or Evelyn. He'd tried to kill me, too, and he'd had me beaten up.

But I didn't think any of that mattered much.

To me he was still Ray, my friend, the black kid I'd grown up with. Looking at it from his point of view, I could see that he'd never really been my equal, not in the eyes of a lot of other people. Dino and I had gotten most of the ink for our athletic prowess, and maybe that was because we were white. And Ray had fetched and carried for Dino for a long time, while Dino seemed to expect no less. There was a depth of bitterness in Ray from past years that I knew I would never understand.

So I didn't want to kill him.

I'd already killed two men that night, and I wasn't sure I'd ever be able to accept having done so. I never wanted another dead man on my conscience, especially not a dead friend.

But when I got my footing, I fired the pistol anyway.

I wasn't really aiming. I was shaking too hard for that, and I was too exhausted for accuracy. It was all chance, and it was clearly self-defense. Despite all my feelings for Ray, he clearly had no qualms about disposing of me. Right at that moment, I don't think anything would have pleased him more.

"I hate your goddammed soul, Tru!" he screamed as he fired for the third time.

The bullet went wild. I didn't even hear it hit the water. He was taking aim again when I pulled the trigger of the Mauser.

Ray seemed to rise out of the water. "Shit," he said, sounding more surprised than anything.

Then he sank under the surface.

"Ray!" I said. I pushed forward, trying to get to him.

It took me a minute, but I reached the place where he'd gone under. Stuffing the pistol in my pants, I dived after him.

He was right there. I pulled him to the surface and started for the shore. It wasn't far. I towed him with my hand under his chin, and he floated in my wake, relaxed now, all the hate gone out of him.

I got him out on the shore and tried to make him comfortable. I knew that he must be freezing in the wind. "I'll get help, Ray," I said. "It won't take long."

"Never mind . . . that," Ray said. I was surprised he could speak. There was a hole in his shirt, right in the center of his chest. "I could never be a pro . . . could I? Screwed up . . . again. I . . . I'm sorry, Tru, about . . . everything."

I stood up from where I'd been kneeling in the sand beside him. "Don't be sorry," I said. "We're all still alive. I think."

"Not . . . all," he said. "I'm sorry about . . . Jan."

19

THERE WAS NO ONE on the seawall except me.

I didn't know where the rat was. I'd gone there to look for him, but he was nowhere around. Not that I blamed him.

It was cold and gray, with a stinging rain in the air being blown along by what was probably the season's last really strong norther. The boulevard was wet and shiny in the lights from the few cars that drove by.

I was carrying a blue cardboard box of Kraft American cheese. I'd brought it for the rat. I don't know why I thought I could find him. He was probably warm and dry in some hole among the granite boulders, chewing on the remains of a hermit crab.

I, on the other hand, was cold and wet and getting wetter all the time.

Ray had died on the shore that night. The last word he said was my sister's name. I don't suppose I'll ever know for sure what he meant by it. I hope he meant that he was sorry I'd never found her, but that might not be what he meant at all. It may be that he was out to punish both me and Dino for whatever imagined slights he'd conjured up and that he knew very well what had happened to Jan. It may be that he'd made it happen.

But I'll go on hoping that he didn't and that someday I'll find her or that eventually I'll know the truth about what happened, even if it's a hard truth.

One thing was for sure: Ray was never going to tell. I tried CPR, slapping, screaming, and beating him on the face. He just lay there in the dark and wind.

I finally left him there and hobbled back to the house. Dino had things pretty well under control there, thanks mostly to Evelyn.

Dino managed to get Hobbes to drop the gun, but that was about all he was up to. Hobbes got on top of Dino, digging his thumbs into the reopened wound, when Evelyn realized what was going on, left Sharon, found the pistol, and clobbered Hobbes in the back of the head with it.

She didn't mess around. Hobbes was in the hospital for three days with a severely cracked skull before he finally came around enough to tell the cops his version of what had happened.

For the rest of us, those three days were spent in varying degrees of comfort. Dino, being who he was, got to stay in the hospital in a much nicer room than the one Hobbes was in. Evelyn and Sharon, who had been only creased by Ray's shot at her, got to go home, thanks to Dino's influence.

I got to go to jail.

After all, I was the one who admitted that I'd killed a man, and it didn't take the police long to match the bullets from my pistol with the ones they'd dug out of one of the guys in the warehouse, the one I'd shot in the chest.

Gerald Barnes didn't like me much. It didn't take him long to work up a really good case of moral fervor and outraged indignation. I let him work on it, and I told him as much of the truth as I could. It was up to somebody else to tell him the rest.

Sharon told most of her story straight, except for the part about the kidnapping being her idea. Ray had told her about her past and lured her to Dino's isolated house. Terry had helped Ray with that part. Ray had gotten to him, promised him a big part of the ransom money, which of course he never collected.

Because Sharon was distraught, and young, her story was pretty convincing. Dino and Evelyn backed her up, and so did I, when I found out what I needed to say.

Hobbes, when he came out of his swoon, didn't contradict her. He really hadn't known what was happening at any point. Ray pointed him in a particular direction, told him what to do, and he did it. His story was, of course, that Ray had personally killed Shelton and Ferguson, Ferguson because he got greedy, and Shelton because Ray had no intention of paying him any of the proceeds from the kidnapping and because a dead Shelton told no tales.

Barnes gave me hell, not that I blamed him much.

"You sorry son of a bitch," he said. "You lied to me that day when you found Shelton's body. Looking for your sister, my ass!" He wasn't very big, but he could get mad with the best of them. His face was very red. "I'd like to tie you to a nylon rope and go trolling for sharks."

I was sitting on a cot in a jail cell at the time, which gave him a superior position. Still, I felt as if I had to say something. "You think if I'd told you the real reason I was looking for Shelton you could have done any better?"

He put his hands on his hips and looked at me. "Maybe," he said.

"Just maybe?"

"Just maybe. But *maybe* your friend Ray would be alive now. *Maybe* your friend Dino wouldn't be in the hospital with bullet holes in him. *Maybe* you wouldn't have killed three men."

I didn't like to think about that last part any more than

I had to. And *maybe* he was right. But he could have been wrong. If I hadn't mixed in, Sharon could have been dead, and Dino, too. I could have been dead for that matter.

I got the feeling in fact that Barnes would have been happier if Ray had killed me instead of vice versa, but that was all right. He'd get over it. What was really bothering him was that I'd solved his murder case, on which he'd made absolutely no progress, and he liked to think that he could have done just as well as I had if I'd given him all the information. He might even have been right, but it didn't make much difference now.

Evelyn came by to tell me that Sharon was holding up pretty well, considering all that had happened to her. They let us meet in the visitors' room.

"She knows how wrong she was," Evelyn said. "And she blames herself for everything."

"She shouldn't," I said. "Ray was just waiting for something. He would have made a move sooner or later, no matter what. And he would have made it on Sharon. Believe me."

"How can you be so sure of that?"

I hadn't told anyone about Ray's dying words, and I didn't intend to. That was my business. Mine and Ray's. "I'm just sure," I said. "That's all. You can tell Sharon that. If she thinks she had a rotten break, tell her a little about Ray. She's still got a chance. Ray hasn't."

"I'll tell her," she said.

She asked what else she could do, and I asked her to call Vicky. Vicky came by the jail not too long after that.

"Nice place," she said. "You trying to impress me?"

"Sure," I said. "All the best people stay here. You selling any soap?"

"A little," she said. She was wearing the pink workout suit again. "I didn't realize what a dangerous man you were."

Her tone was light, but there was something in her eyes that showed me she meant it.

"I don't mean to be," I said. "Things just worked out that way."

"Ms. Matthews made it sound as if you were hurt."

"It's just an old football injury," I said. I told her about the knee and how it got that way.

"You mean you were almost an all-American?"

"Yeah," I said. "Almost."

We talked for a bit longer, and she agreed to go by the house and look after Nameless. It turned out that she was a cat lover.

"You won't love this one," I said. "He's not very affection-ate."

"Sort of like his owner?"

"I can be very affectionate. In the right circumstances. These aren't the right circumstances."

"I see what you mean. Can we discuss this after you get out of here?"

"Absolutely," I said. Then I told her where my spare key was hidden and asked her to go up to the bedroom and bring me the copy of *Absalom, Absalom*, the Faulkner book that I'd been reading. I figured I'd have plenty of time to finish it now.

She brought it back later that day. "I read this one time, in an English class," she said. "It was all right, but I didn't like the way it ended."

"I'll let you know what I think. What about the cat?"

"He was very sweet. Sitting right by the porch as if he were waiting for me. Rubbed all around my legs while I was unlocking the door."

"He didn't try to scratch you?"

"Of course not. I gave him a good rub after I fed him. You ought to pet him more."

"I'll give it a try."

"I'll be back tomorrow," she said.

*   *   *

It took three days for Dino's lawyer to get through all the roadblocks Barnes threw in his way, including one of Barnes's pet judges, but he finally got me out. He assured me that with Hobbes's testimony and the statements from Sharon, Dino, and Evelyn, I wouldn't have to go back to the jail, at least not for anything that had happened recently.

"It's clearly all self-defense," he said. "I'm sure that all charges will be dropped and that you won't even have to appear before the grand jury." He was a young man in a sharp suit that he hadn't bought at the mall. I figured that he must know what he was talking about.

By the time I was released, I'd finished *Absalom, Absalom.* It bothered me more than I wanted to tell anyone, and I hoped Vicky wouldn't ask me about it. Colonel Sutpen's son, tainted by the wrong blood, denied by his father, eventually killed by his half-brother—it all reminded me a little too much of Ray and Dino. And even a little bit of myself. Goodhue Coldfield, living out his life in his attic and dying there, well, at least Dino and Sally West hadn't retreated that far yet. Not quite. I left the book in the cell. Maybe the next inmate would find it more enlightening than I had. Or less.

I went by the hospital to see Dino, who was ready to leave. "It's not too bad here now," he said. "I got a TV, at least." He pointed to the color set that was held high on the wall opposite his bed on some sort of metal holder. The controls were pinned to his bed. "I'll have some more money for you when I get out of this place."

"Don't worry about the money," I said.

"I know what you mean," he said. "Old Ray." He shook his head. "I've been thinking about what he said, you know? And what worries me is that he might even have been right. I mean, I did order him around a lot. But hell, I did that with everybody. When you grow up like I did, you get to thinking it's all right. I'd even forgotten that I'd asked him to pick up some beers on the night of that wreck. I'm not the one who caused it, though. That wasn't my fault." He looked around the hospital room. "Or was it?"

I couldn't help him there. I was wondering how much of it was mine. "What about you and Evelyn?" I said.

"What does that mean?"

I felt awkward. "I don't know. I just thought, well, maybe the two of you . . ." I didn't know how to finish.

Dino reached for the TV control and fiddled with it. I could tell he wanted to turn the set on, but he resisted.

"I don't know," he said finally. "All those years. You were right about me. I was one step from being a hermit. But it wouldn't be easy to change. Not now. I'm not too sure about Sharon, either. I don't think she likes me very much. This whole thing wouldn't have happened if she hadn't wanted to get back at me. It wouldn't be easy to make up for all those years."

I didn't try to reassure him the way I had Evelyn. "I see what you mean," I said.

"Yeah. And Evelyn, she's OK, and she saved my ass twice, but I'm not sure that she'd want me around all the time. There'd be a lot of talk."

I laughed. "There was a lot of talk before, remember. I'm sure half the town knew about you and Evelyn. And these days no one would be surprised by anything. If you two got together, it wouldn't make a ripple. People have got a lot more to talk about than your love life."

Dino managed a wry grin. "You may be right about that. My family's not exactly front-page news around the Island anymore."

"You must not have seen a paper lately," I said.

"Sure I have, and you'll notice that I was able to keep most of what happened out of it. It was just an ordinary kidnapping as far as anyone knows."

"Don't count on that," I said. I was thinking about Sally

West. "Not everyone gets the news from the papers. But in a week or two, everyone will be talking about something else. There's nothing as boring as old news."

"I guess so," he said. "Still . . ."

I left it like that. What Dino did with his life was his own business, and maybe Evelyn and Sharon's business, but it wasn't mine. Not any longer.

I left the hospital and bought a bottle of Mogen David. Then I drove to Sally West's home and told her the whole thing, more or less unedited.

"You know," she said, taking a sip of the sweet wine, "hearing that story almost makes me feel young again." She sipped again. "Almost."

"Not me," I said. "It makes me feel a hundred years old."

"You don't remember the old days," she said. "Not the way I do, at any rate. Dino's uncles were always living on the edge. Oh, not of kidnapping or anything like that, but it made life on the Island exciting. The place had personality then, even if it did mean that the Texas Rangers were always trying to close things down. It could be that way again, you know."

"I wouldn't want it to be," I said. "Not if it meant doing what I've had to do."

"No, I suppose you wouldn't." She sipped. "What do you suppose Ray meant by that remark?"

I didn't have to ask her which remark she meant. She was the only one I'd told about what Ray said just before he died.

"I don't know," I said. "Maybe someday I'll find out."

"You'll be sure to let me know, won't you?"

"You'll be the first," I said.

My sweatshirt was soaked, and the cardboard box holding the cheese had just about turned to mush in my hand, but there was still no sign of the rat.

There was a rumble of thunder, and a gust of wind blew

the rain right through the legs of my running pants.

I looked over the seawall one last time, and I thought I saw a shadow move from one of the granite boulders to the next. The rain slid over their slick pink and black surfaces.

I took the cheese out of the box. Then I mashed up the box and stuck it in my back pocket. No sense in adding to the clutter already there. I peeled the cellophane off the cheese and put the cellophane in my pocket with the box.

"That you down there, rat?" I said.

There was no answer, but of course I hadn't really expected one. I tossed the eight ounces of cheese down to where I'd seen the shadow move, turned, and jogged away.

The rain stung my face, but my knee hardly hurt at all.

If you have enjoyed this book and would like to receive details on other Walker mysteries, please write to:

Mystery Editor
Walker and Company
720 Fifth Avenue
New York, NY 10019